Blaze™

Bestselling author Tori Carrington introduces
Private Scandals, a new miniseries
filled with lust, betrayal...and scandal
like you've never seen it!

When Troy, Ari and Bryna Metaxas realize
their business—and family—is on the brink of
ruin, how far will they go to save them?

Find out in...

Private Sessions
(October 2010)

Private Affairs
(November 2010)

Private Parts
(December 2010)

Private Scandals—
Nothing remains hidden for long....

Dear Reader,

There's just something about a strong, bad-boy hero who can rock a business suit, isn't there? He may try to conceal his true character, but once you get this guy between the sheets...oh, my!

Private Sessions is the first in our three-book Private Scandals series and focuses on hot businessman Caleb Payne, who embodies all of what bad boys are made of. He knows exactly what it takes to get what he wants—especially when it comes to sexy Bryna Metaxas, who not only provides an opportunity to glean a bit of enjoyment from the disaster that is Caleb's current business life, but to exact a bit of revenge. But there are some sins that are unforgivable.... Has he finally gone too far?

We hope you enjoy every sizzling, heart-stopping moment of Caleb and Bryna's journey toward happily-ever-after. We'd love to hear what you think. Contact us at P.O. Box 12271, Toledo, OH 43612 (we'll respond with a signed bookplate, newsletter and bookmark), or visit us on the Web at www.toricarrington.net.

Here's wishing you love, romance and HOT reading.

Lori & Tony Karayianni
aka Tori Carrington

Tori Carrington

PRIVATE SESSIONS

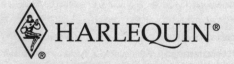

HARLEQUIN®

TORONTO • NEW YORK • LONDON
AMSTERDAM • PARIS • SYDNEY • HAMBURG
STOCKHOLM • ATHENS • TOKYO • MILAN • MADRID
PRAGUE • WARSAW • BUDAPEST • AUCKLAND

Recycling programs
for this product may
not exist in your area.

ISBN-13: 978-0-373-79572-7

PRIVATE SESSIONS

This edition published by arrangement with Harlequin Books S.A.

For questions and comments about the quality of this book please contact us at Customer_eCare@Harlequin.ca.

® and TM are trademarks of the publisher. Trademarks indicated with ® are registered in the United States Patent and Trademark Office, the Canadian Trade Marks Office and in other countries.

www.eHarlequin.com

Printed in U.S.A.

ABOUT THE AUTHOR

Multi-award-winning, bestselling authors Lori Schlachter Karayianni and Tony Karayianni are the power behind the pen name Tori Carrington. Their more than forty-five titles include numerous Harlequin Blaze miniseries, as well as the ongoing Sofie Metropolis comedic mystery series with another publisher. Visit www.toricarrington.net and www.sofiemetro.com for more information on the duo and their titles.

Books by Tori Carrington

Don't miss any of our special offers. Write to us at the following address for information on our newest releases.

Harlequin Reader Service
U.S.: 3010 Walden Ave., P.O. Box 1325, Buffalo, NY 14269
Canadian: P.O. Box 609, Fort Erie, Ont. L2A 5X3

We dedicate this book to bad-boy-loving
women everywhere....

And to Julie Chivers and editor extraordinaire
Brenda Chin: you guys rock!

Prologue

"GREAT SEX IS NOT ENOUGH for me, Caleb. Not anymore."

Damn. There it was...

Caleb Payne stood in front of the floor-to-ceiling windows of his penthouse apartment, his attention not on the reflection of the beautiful woman who had uttered the words, but on the sight beyond the glass. Seattle's skyline twinkled against the inky late-night backdrop. His fingers tightened around the crystal tumbler that held an inch of the best whiskey the civilized world had to offer. He downed the smooth liquid in one swallow and then slowly dragged the back of his hand against his mouth, finally considering Cissy's image in the window.

How was it possible such an attractive woman suddenly emerged unappealing? Despite the low-cut, curve-hugging long red dress she wore, her white-blond hair floating around her smooth shoulders, he wanted to look everywhere but at her.

His gaze fell to her full breasts. Correction: he wanted to look everywhere but into her pleading, hopeful face.

She instinctively crossed her arms, impeding his view.

"Sex is all I have to give you." Caleb slowly turned, considering her reaction from beneath his brows. "I told you that from the beginning."

He'd seen this coming since earlier that evening, when his limo had stopped at her downtown apartment to pick her up for the charity ball they'd attended.

Actually, if he were honest, he'd seen this coming since the day they'd first met.

It gave him no pleasure to know that he'd been spot-on when it came to the timeline he'd imagined when he'd met the pretty socialite six months ago. Around about month three, she'd started talking exclusivity. Which hadn't been a problem, considering it was in his cautious nature to stick to one sexual partner at a time. Month four brought talk of combining households, a conversation he'd artfully avoided.

And tonight, a week before the end of month six, she had launched her plan for even more.

"I've never lied to you, Cissy," he told her now. "You knew the score from the beginning."

"But things change. People change."

He shook his head. "Not me. Never me."

Pain crumpled her face, an emotion that left him unmoved.

He wondered if she'd say the words countless others had said before her and call him a heartless bastard.

If she did, she'd be right. He'd been raised by a single mother, never knowing his father although the man had always been nearby, present without being a presence. While Caleb had never wanted for anything materially…well, one therapist he'd dated had suggested he'd been stunted emotionally by his upbringing.

He'd been a bastard child within a socio-economic class that still frowned heavily on such things. And his peers had never let him forget it.

That's where the heartless part entered in.

Oh, Cissy might want more now, but in a week, maybe two, she'd be thankful she hadn't been successful in her efforts. Out there somewhere was a man who would improve her standing; not detract from it.

He walked to the bar and poured another finger into his glass, waiting for the other shoe to drop.

"Is marriage anywhere in the cards for us?" Cissy asked quietly.

He inwardly winced.

Once, just once, he'd like to be proven wrong. He'd like to date a woman who was unpredictable. Someone who would surprise him. Someone who'd enjoy whatever moments they could spend together without planning, scheming, plotting for something more.

Someone who wouldn't want something he was incapable of giving.

He shook his head. "No."

He heard her moving around. Imagined her picking up her wrap. Checking inside her purse. Perhaps getting a tissue with which to wipe her nose. Then stalking toward the front door.

"Well, then, I guess this is goodbye." Her voice was half accusatory, half hopeful.

He nodded again without turning. "Goodbye, Cissy."

Silence. Long moments later the door closed behind her. Caleb downed the whiskey, tapping his fingers against the expensive crystal. Shame. He'd liked Cissy. She'd been nice to have around. Nice to have in his bed.

He sighed and then headed for his home office and the only thing that never asked him for anything more, that never complained or questioned or demanded, or failed to hold his fascination: work.

1

THE MORE THINGS CHANGED, the more they stayed the same.

Bryna Metaxas weighed the old axiom, feeling exasperated by her job, by the current stagnancy of her love life—or, rather, the lack of one at all—and frustrated by everything in general.

She sat in her small office at the old lumber mill where Metaxas Limited was located in Earnest, Washington, blind to the view of the lush, pine-covered hills visible through the window behind her. She was too busy trying not to think about the weekly Tuesday meeting she'd attended that morning where she'd been marginalized yet again. She couldn't help wondering why her older cousin Troy included her if he wasn't going to have her do anything more substantial than take notes and follow up on minor details. She was half-surprised that he hadn't asked her to serve coffee to the dozen attendees while they brainstormed ideas on where to go now that the deal they'd been working on with Greek billionaire Manolis Philippidis had fallen through.

Fallen through. Now, that was a print-ready description for what had happened. *Disaster* would be more fitting.

Bryna drew in a deep breath. How long had she been working at the company? Nearly two years. And while every six months she was given a positive review and her salary was increased incrementally, she was doing basically the same mundane tasks she had done since the day she hired on.

At any other company she would have quit long ago. But this was a family operation…and she was part of the family.

Besides, as a resident of Earnest, she had a vested interest in seeing the plan succeed for the good of the community. Hell, she'd minored in green energy at university and had a better working knowledge of the emerging technology than either of her cousins.

Bryna sighed and pushed her straight black hair back from her face. On her desk sat three different versions of a proposal—variants on the original she'd put together months ago, but had never seen the top of her cousin's in-box. A proposal she'd thought stood a chance when the Philippidis debacle happened. But, no. If anything, Troy was even less interested in looking at her ideas. No matter how many bricks walls he continually ran into.

Ultimately, she'd decided she'd have to fly solo.

It was just after eleven and she'd been at the old family mill offices since six, moths fluttering their wings against the walls of her stomach at the thought of going this alone. If some of that wild flapping was also associated with the very attractive person she'd decided to approach first…well, she wasn't admitting to it, beyond allowing that it had been a while since she'd enjoyed male attention…and this particular hot, single male not only appeared skilled in that specific area, he was renowned for it.

At any rate, if her plan worked the way she hoped, she'd be a major player in the business rather than the second fiddle to which she'd been relegated.

Of course, if her cousins Troy and his younger brother Ari found out what she was up to, they'd probably fire her sorry butt on the spot, family ties be damned.

She heard Troy's voice in the hall outside her door. Bryna quickly put another file on top of the proposals and picked up a pen, pretending interest in the routine accounting job she'd been given to do the day before.

"Hey, Bry," Troy said, leaning against the door-jamb the way he always did.

Everything that the gossips said about both of her cousins was true. They were powerful and impossibly good-looking, walking, talking Greek gods, a double whammy to any single female within grinning distance.

Of course, Ari was no longer on the market. And Troy...

"You look like shit," she said.

And he did. It was the height of summer and he looked pale as a ghost. And tired beyond what any amount of sleep could cure.

The reason for that was closely tied into Ari's change in bachelor status. A month ago the two brothers had traveled to Greece, not so much for the Philippidis wedding, but to close the deal with the wealthy groom that would put the company on a fast track. And save Earnest, the old mill town that they all called home that had recently chalked up a twenty-five percent unemployment rate, the highest in its hundred-year history.

Needless to say, the deal hadn't gone through. Not through any fault of Troy's. Rather, Ari's infatuation with the bride had resulted in the collapse of not only the deal, but contributed to the downward spiral of what was left of the company itself.

And that broke Bryna's heart. Metaxas Limited was a true family business. Troy...well, what would he do without the company his grandfather and then father built? He lived, ate and breathed ML. The cash flow reflected his blood flow.

Both Troy and Ari were much more than cousins to her: they were her brothers. She'd been an only child until she was twelve and the Cessna her father had been flying had crashed, killing him and her mother as they'd been returning from a weekend trip to San Francisco. Her father's brother had generously provided a home for her along with his two sons, his own wife having died long ago.

It hadn't been easy being the only female in a house full of males. But it had been interesting. She remembered the first time she'd brought a boy home to "study," when she was fifteen. Troy and Ari had invited Dale Whitman out back for a talk after they'd caught him and Bryna enjoying a first kiss over their chemistry books. When Dale hadn't returned to the dining room within ten minutes, she went looking for him. And found him trussed up by his ankles, suspended from a branch of the old oak tree out back.

Her cousins had scared him so badly that not only had he not returned, no other boyfriend had dared show up at the Metaxas estate again, the ankle story having taken on a life of its own and grown to mythological proportions that would do the Greeks proud.

And this company was their Mount Olympus.

Which is why Bryna had decided it was long past time she took action to defend and protect the same.

Her cousin chuckled quietly at her comment and rubbed his freshly shaven chin. "Gee, thanks. Exactly what I needed to hear this morning."

Bryna grimaced. "Just calling 'em as I see 'em."

"Yeah, well, maybe that's one of the reasons why you haven't earned that promotion you've been angling for."

"Oh, so unfair. I'm speaking to you cousin to cousin now. Not employer to employee."

"And the difference in the Land of Bryna?"

She flashed him a bright smile. "I'd be much nicer if we weren't related."

She successfully concealed her true reaction to her recent promotion denial. She wanted to be included on an equal level, damn it. Was that too much to ask? Okay, so she was only twenty-four. But she'd graduated summa cum laude from WSU with her master's in business administration. And she was up to the task.

She'd even told them she didn't need a hike in salary. Just give her anything that was above junior associate, essentially a glorified office assistant, and she'd be happy.

Troy had told her no. Again. That the company was putting a freeze on all promotions for the time being.

She'd half expected him to ruffle her hair and tell her to go out and play like a good girl.

She needed to convince him that she wasn't their cute little cousin anymore. Or merely their cute little cousin; she had no intention of giving up her special spot in the family.

Troy said, "If that were true, I'd give you the promotion in a blink."

She twisted her lips. "I'm never going to live down that Bainwright incident, am I?"

"Bainwright incident? Oh, wait. Yes, now I remember." He shook his finger at her. "Maybe it's just me, but dumping the contents of a water pitcher in a supplier's lap during a meeting is not exactly good work etiquette."

"Neither is his copping a feel while I was pouring his water."

"He said it was an honest mistake."

"An honest mistake would be if he'd removed the hand in question the moment it made contact. Not leave it there and give a couple of squeezes for good measure."

She remembered the slimy man's fingers on her breast and gave an involuntary shudder.

Troy sighed heavily. "When you realize that perhaps you could have handled the situation more diplomatically, maybe then we'll have another talk about that promotion."

Bryna sat back, prepared to say something along the lines of "So I suppose offering him my other breast for a tweak would have been preferable."

Instead, her gaze fell on the files on her desk. More specifically, on the proposals that she was scheduled to pitch to none other than Manolis Philippidis's principal consultant in…

"Oh, my God, is that the time?" Bryna launched herself from her chair.

Troy blinked at her. "What, do you have an appointment?"

"Yes," she confirmed, pulling on her suit jacket and buttoning the front. "Yes, I do."

"May I ask with whom?"

She struck a pose. "With the hairdresser in Seattle. Would you like to attend, act as my wingman?"

He chuckled. "Thanks, but I'll pass."

"You may want to rethink that. You could probably use a good spray tan."

She discreetly stuffed the proposals into her brief-case and began to pass him.

"Very funny."

"See you later, then."

"Since it's Tuesday, why don't you just stay there? Come back on Sunday?"

Her usual schedule was to head to her small apart-ment in Seattle every Wednesday night, spend two days working from there, then return home to the Metaxas estate Sunday morning for brunch, starting the cycle over again.

"No, I'll be coming back this afternoon," she told him.

As Bryna headed toward the old steel stairs and the parking lot beyond the mill doors, she wasn't sure which bothered her more: that she was nervous as hell, or that Troy hadn't even thought twice about her leaving in the middle of the morning.

Just went to show you how much her cousin really thought of her and her work ethic.

She smiled to herself. If everything went the way she planned, that would all change soon enough....

2

To the victor the spoils....

Caleb knew who Bryna Metaxas was. She was related to the same man indirectly responsible for the collapse of his latest business deal. But given the fact that his position or personal wealth hadn't been impacted, he was still the victor.

And she was very definitely the spoils. Because he had absolutely no interest in pursuing anything of a business nature with her.

They'd met once. During a meeting at Metaxas Limited. While Manolis Philippidis had droned on about a catch in the contract, Caleb had allowed himself to appreciate Bryna's remarkable beauty. The type of looker who would be right at home sunning herself on one of Philippidis's yachts, a white, barely there bikini playing up her physical assets, large sunglasses perched on her petite nose, her long, dark hair combed back while a formally clad waiter served her a dirty martini. He remembered thinking that she could easily challenge any of the goddesses her Greek ancestry boasted on the sexy meter. Why she would ever want to be associated with her loser cousins was an intriguing mystery to him. Especially since whatever ideas she'd proffered were immediately squashed by her cousin Troy, her thoughtful frown as he did so making her all the more appealing.

And she looked even better now, staring up at him with a wide smile.

Although for the record he'd prefer to see her in that barely there bikini rather than in the too-stern navy blue suit she had on.

He openly appreciated the pretty young woman who'd stormed his office after he'd made her wait for half an hour. She was a little on the young side. He was maybe a decade her senior. But if his recent experiences had taught him anything, it was that seeing women closer to his own age came with baggage he was no longer interested in carrying. Biological clocks and measuring sticks were tucked in their designer handbags, always nearby, always dictating their actions.

Bryna was young and had yet to hear the distant ticking. And her handbag of choice appeared to be a briefcase.

The fact that she was a member of the Metaxas family added a certain illicit appeal to her attraction quotient. It had been Ari Metaxas who sank one of his prized deals. Oh, not the business proposal that bit the dust with Philippidis's marriage plans. But the contract Caleb had been working on for two years with a Dubai company that would have resulted in one of the largest conglomerates currently operating today.

The same contract that Philippidis's single-minded lust for revenge against Metaxas and his unfaithful bride had mucked up beyond repair.

"Thanks for taking my appointment," Bryna said, moving her briefcase from one hand to the other and then extending her right.

"No problem." Was her skin really that soft? Caleb shamelessly held on to the feminine digits, rubbing his thumb slowly along the back.

He watched her pupils grow large in her dark green irises at the unabashed liberty he took. But rather than immediately try to pull away, she held his gaze, allowing the fiery spark that ignited between them to flare, running from her skin over to his. The heat sped downward and settled pleasantly in his groin.

He allowed himself a moment to imagine removing that barely there bikini in his fantasy to leave her fully bare…

Bryna cleared her throat and slowly withdrew her hand, taking the sexy image with her.

"I have three proposals I'd like to submit to you," she said, sitting in one of the two high-backed visitor's chairs and putting her case down at her crossed ankles. Slender, shapely ankles that drew his attention.

She took documents out of her briefcase and held them out to him.

He made no move to take them. Instead, he permitted his gaze to rake up her calves to where the hem of her skirt had hiked up to just above her pleasing knees.

Bryna placed the proposals on the desk he stood next to.

"I'm sure that once you've had a chance to review them, you'll see that a partnership with Metaxas Limited would be in everyone's best interest."

Having her open her knees a little wider would be in his best interest. Would she be wearing plain white panties, he wondered. Black? Red? Or would she surprise him by going commando?

The idea nudged his temperature gauge up more than a few notches.

He lifted his telltale gaze back to her face. "Does Troy know you're here?"

He'd met both brothers on several occasions, but he'd gotten the distinct impression that the elder was in charge of all business dealings. And a control freak. Much like he, himself, was.

He was intrigued by the way Bryna avoided his gaze.

If he were to guess, he'd say that no one was aware that she was there.

Caleb knew himself well enough to recognize his growing attraction to the young woman sitting in his visitor's chair. And judging by her reaction when they'd touched, he knew it would be all too easy to draw her into a sexual liaison. A few carefully placed caresses, whispered words, and she'd melt like butter on his toast.

The telecom buzzed.

His secretary. He'd instructed her to interrupt the meeting at minute five.

The problem lay in that he wasn't all too sure he wanted to end his time with Bryna Metaxas.

"Excuse me," he said.

"Sure. Go ahead."

He picked up the phone and listened for a moment, his gaze roving hungrily over Bryna's soft curves, before hanging up.

"I'm sorry," he said, going for feigned reluctance and surprised to actually be feeling it. "But there appears to be an overseas call I really must take."

She twisted lips that were full and lush and made for a man's kiss. "Of course." She got up from the chair. "I'm grateful for the time you've extended me. Just give my office a call when you've had a chance to review the proposals so we can set up another meeting." She began to turn away, then lifted a finger and swiveled back. Her mouth was slightly open, as if prepared to say something, but his expression—which he was sure revealed his naked interest in her—must have caused her to hesitate.

Her pink tongue darted out and moistened those provocative lips.

"Actually," she said quietly, then cleared her throat, "I'll, um, call you."

Caleb found himself crossing the room to be nearer to her. The musky scent of her perfume filled his senses. He dragged his gaze away from her mouth up to her eyes and then crossed his arms over his chest, as much to keep from touching her as to maintain the distance he wasn't sure why he suddenly required. "Why did you choose me, Miss Metaxas?"

She was clearly as aware of him as he was of her…and thrown by his close proximity. He watched her elegant throat work around a swallow. "I don't understand?"

"Why didn't you go straight to Philippidis himself?"

Her smile was soft, tinged with a bit of wryness. "I thought my chances of putting together something with you were better, considering the circumstances." She took in the width of his shoulders, his height. "I mean, you're an independent consultant, right? While you're associated with Philippidis, you're not his employee." She shrugged, the action looking anything but nonchalant. "We can't sell Philippidis, but perhaps we—you and I—can work together to sell the idea to someone else."

He liked her confidence…her awareness of herself as a woman. And he admired her poise; obviously she'd put a lot of thought into her approach, even though she knew the chances of him taking her up on her offer were remote.

He picked up the folders, glanced at the top one, then held them out to her.

"While flattered, Miss Metaxas, I'm afraid I'm not interested."

Inaccurate to the nth degree. The problem lay in that he was very interested in her…only on a much more personal level.

She hesitantly took the proposals, but the look in her eyes told him that she saw him; possibly saw right through him.

Caleb cocked a brow.

"Are you sure there isn't…something I can do to persuade you differently.…" she asked quietly, leadingly.

He'd been playing the man v. woman game for long enough that he understood some had the killer instinct, were born with a natural understanding of basic human need and how to bend it to their advantage, and some didn't.

Sexy Miss Bryna Metaxas had been born with it. She might not understand exactly how best to use it, but she knew enough to make her very enticing, indeed.

He smiled. "I'm sure."

He drew closer to her, estimating that he had a good five inches on her and years of experience. While she demonstrated good instinctive skills, she was no match for him in any department.

Why, then, did he want to see just how much of challenge she'd present?

He was a breath away from her. She didn't blink. Didn't move. Didn't indicate one way or another if he intimidated her. To the contrary, she appeared equally as enthralled by the chemistry that existed between them.

"I feel it only fair to tell you that this won't be the last you hear from me," she said so quietly it was nearly a whisper.

Caleb's gaze slid over her face, taking in the hint of heated color and her decadent mouth before returning to her eyes.

"I certainly hope not, Miss Metaxas."

He watched as she gave him one last smile and then turned to leave. He stood for long moments after the door closed behind her.

Fascinating.

He walked back behind his desk and picked up the phone to ask his secretary to place a call for him. Then noticed that the sly bird had left the proposals on his desk despite his handing them back to her.

He grinned, giving her points for moxie.

And scoring her highly across the board...

3

BRYNA SAT IN HER CAR in the parking lot of Metaxas Limited. Despite the routine forty-five-minute drive from the city back to Earnest, she felt oddly shaken, as if she'd just escaped being run down by a speeding car…and she wanted to step right back into its path.

She'd heard that Caleb Payne was not a man to fool around with. And when their paths had crossed before she'd certainly seen firsthand that he could be darkly suggestive. But this morning…wow. She couldn't have been more affected by him had he lit a flamethrower and aimed it in her direction. Even now her skin tingled and her panties were damp from their brief face-to-face. Oh, his words may have been straightforward and dismissive. But his dark eyes had held wicked invitation. One that she found she wanted to take him up on, despite all the bells and whistles going off warning her against just that.

Okay, so maybe it wasn't a good idea to be entertaining thoughts of seducing the man she wanted to help pull Metaxas Limited back from the brink. If she were being honest, it was a very bad idea. She'd never mixed business with pleasure before and now, with the stakes as high as they were, she shouldn't even be thinking about it.

Which was probably part of the reason she was.

Her younger cousin Ari had once told her that she had a dangerous streak to her. Opting to date the bad boys over the good. Taking imprudent risks with her job that found her struggling for acceptance and advancement.

She closed her eyes tightly, both hands gripping the steering wheel, and took a deep breath.

Go away, go away, go away, she ordered the image of Caleb Payne etched into the back of her eyelids.

A knock on her window caused her to knock her head against the roof of her late-model Mustang GT. Which was no less than she deserved, she thought wryly as she stared out at Ari standing next to her car.

She slid the keys from the ignition and opened the door too fast, hitting his legs.

"Ow." Ari chuckled as he stepped back. "Sorry. I didn't mean to startle you."

Bryna pushed the door lock on her key fob twice, engaging the alarm. "That's why you knocked on the window and gave me a robin's egg on my head."

"A robin's egg?" He lifted his hand to touch her hair and she playfully batted it out of the way.

"Don't you dare."

His grin was one-hundred-percent pure Ari.

When it came to the charm and looks departments, it was joked within the family that Ari Metaxas had hit the genetic lottery. If he smiled at you, you were required to smile back. It was as simple as that.

That it had been that same irresistible charm that had landed the company in trouble wasn't surprising.

"Where you coming back from?" Ari asked as they walked toward the offices.

"I should be asking you the same thing."

"I asked you first."

"So you did." Abruptly, Bryna had a hard time remembering her excuse for being away from the office.

She absently rubbed at the bump on her head and then remembered. A hair appointment. Yes, that was it.

"Salon," she told him. "And you?"

"Lunch with my fiancée."

Bryna tried not to let her feelings register in a visual way, but Ari must have caught her frown.

"Uh-oh," he said quietly, his smile vanishing. "Are you still having trouble accepting that Elena and I are together?"

Bryna opened the door for him. "Did I say anything?"

"You didn't have to. It's written all over your face."

All right. So she might have to forgive her cousin for his tawdry behavior. It was an unwritten rule in the familial contract. But the woman at least half—if not fully—responsible for what had happened a month ago in Greece...well, it didn't say anywhere that she couldn't hold a grudge against her for life.

"She's carrying my child. Your niece or nephew."

Bryna softened. He hadn't said *second cousin,* which was actually what would be the case. But *niece or nephew.* Her heart expanded with fondness.

This was exactly the reason it was easy to forgive Ari's charming little heart.

"How'd the doctor's appointment go?" she asked.

Ari's grin made a bouncing comeback. "I heard the baby's heartbeat. It has to be the second-best thing I've ever heard in my life."

"Second?"

"Elena's soft sighs are the first."

Bryna held up her hand palm out. "TMI."

"Get your mind out of the gutter, Bry."

They climbed the steps to the second floor of the old mill offices and walked down the narrow hallway. "Who says my mind's in the gutter?"

She would. Ever since the meeting with Caleb.

"TMI includes mushy sweet moments, as well."

"Ah, I get it."

She walked through the open doorway to her office and then turned toward him. "Don't you have some work to do?"

He slid his hands into the pockets of his khaki pants, his crisp, navy blazer draping back in a way that made him look as if he'd just stepped from a Calvin Klein ad.

He opened his mouth to say something and she closed her door in his face, staring at him through the glass.

He laughed and shook his head, continuing on down the hall toward his own office.

Bryna placed her briefcase on her desk, then opened the door again, looking up and down the hallway. She didn't see one of the dozen people who worked there.

Good. She needed a few moments to herself to get her thoughts together.

And to scheme exactly how she was going to sneak a meeting with Caleb Payne again…one that might include indulging in the vivid fantasies that were forming in her mind at the mere idea of acting on the intense attraction that existed between them.…

As MUCH A LONER AS HE WAS, he hated eating alone.

Caleb lingered in his office after five o'clock that Friday, checking his watch and thinking about whom he could invite to dinner at such a late hour. Someone who wouldn't expect anything beyond a good meal. He wasn't up to anything more.

He had a couple of male colleagues he could call, but both were married. And while the thought of eating alone didn't please him, less appealing was dining solo at a couple's house. Especially a young couple convinced they were in love.

"Mr. Payne?"

His secretary opened the door after briefly knocking.

"I have the New York attorney for you on line one."

Caleb looked at his watch. That would make it after 8:00 p.m. eastern time. Which was pretty much par for the course for their conversations. He didn't hire anyone who wasn't two hundred percent committed to their careers.

"Thank you, Nancy. Any word yet on Manolis?"

Philippidis had been avoiding his calls all day.

"No, sir. I'm still trying."

"Thank you."

She left the office, closing the door behind her. He turned his attention to the waiting call from his personal attorney.

How long had this case been dragging on? Two years? And the last time he checked, it was no closer to being resolved than when he originally brought the suit.

Of course, the unusual nature of his petition was partly responsible. Most courts didn't know what to do with a thirty-two-year-old man's request to force a DNA test. Especially when the parent in question was deceased.

"Harry," Caleb said, picking up the extension.

"Caleb."

He sat back in the chair and closed his eyes; he could tell by the sound of the attorney's voice that this wasn't going to be good.

"I've received an offer."

He listened as an amount in the mid-seven digits was named.

"Are you still there?" Harry asked, reminding him that he had yet to respond.

"No."

A slight pause and then, "No, you're not there? Or, no, no deal?"

He sighed and sat up straighter. "This has never been about the money."

Money he had. In spades. He'd made three times more than his father ever had by age thirty. And the Payne family was just as old and wealthy a New England clan as the Winsteads.

The thought brought his mother's face to mind. As her only child, they'd always shared an especially close bond…drawn tighter, he suspected, by the details surrounding his birth.

He had yet to tell her he was pursuing this lawsuit; of course, that meant little—she was probably already well aware of what was going on. The upper one percent was like a small town with lots of acreage. Still, she had yet to say anything to him. He suspected she was waiting for him to come to her and allowing him to do what he needed to do.

The way he saw it, he was doing this as much for her as for himself. She'd sacrificed so much for him...surely he owed her at least the return of her good name.

"They're anxious for you to let this go."

Of course they were. The Winsteads didn't want an illegitimate child to sully up the late, great Theodore Winstead's good name.

He realized he was gritting his teeth and forced himself to stop.

"You don't have to make a decision now. Sleep on it. I'll call again on Monday."

"No need," Caleb said. "Refuse and go to the next step."

"Will do." Not even a hesitation.

Satisfied, he hung up the phone and sat back again, his every muscle coiled and tense.

He didn't know how long he sat like that until there was another knock and Nancy appeared in the door.

"Any luck finding Philippidis?" he asked.

"No."

He stared at her for minute. It was understood that when he was in the office she was to be present, as well. Unless she requested otherwise, or he dismissed her.

"These messages came in while you were on the phone."

He rubbed his face, noting the stubble there. He'd use his en suite bathroom to shave and clean up before leaving.

He accepted the five slips of paper, leafing through them once, and then again, stopping on one in particular.

He held it up. "Is this her office number?"

"Her cell phone."

Even better.

"Thanks, Nancy. That'll be all. I'll see you on Monday."

"Very good, sir. Good night."

Caleb rounded his desk, waiting until his secretary gathered her things and left the office before sitting down and picking up the phone, dialing the number on the slip.

She picked up on the second ring.

"Our meeting was interrupted the other day. I'd like to continue it."

He waited for Bryna Metaxas to reply. "I'd like that," she said, a low, groin-tightening purr in her voice. "Next week?"

"A half hour. At Giorgio's."

HALF AN HOUR wasn't nearly enough time for a girl to put on her evening best. But when the invitation was accepted, she was bound by business etiquette to follow through.

But as the taxi pulled up to Giorgio's forty minutes later, Bryna knew that business had nothing to do with agreeing to meet Caleb Payne at the upscale restaurant.

She adjusted the heel strap of the gold Grecian-style sandals that Ari had brought back from Santorini for her, paid the driver and stepped out, pleasantly surprised to find Caleb waiting for her outside the doors. She'd expected him to be ensconced in one of the plush booths enjoying a drink, possibly even having ordered already.

Instead he'd waited outside.

Every sensation she'd experienced during their meeting the other day returned...tenfold. She felt... breathless, somehow. Like he was already touching her everywhere she wanted to be touched by him... and she was responding in a greedy, uninhibited way....

Over the past couple of days, she'd tried to convince herself she was overreacting to what had really happened, imagined that he had been attracted to her, shelved any sexual notions with a Post-it that read *harmless flirtation*.

But now she knew she hadn't amplified anything... if anything, she'd downplayed it.

She walked in his direction, watching him watch her. Despite her business argument, she was dressed for sheer pleasure. There was nothing innocent about her choice of little black dress. The clingy material was too intimate, her bare shoulder moist with lotion and perfumed, her hair down from her usual twist and finger-curled around her face.

Bryna hesitated slightly as she drew near enough to speak. In the waning evening light, he looked a dangerous black figure, more shadow than light. And for reasons she was ill-prepared to identify, she felt as if she was walking into a trap. A nicely appointed trap, but one the man across from her had designed to his advantage…and one she fully intended to enter, the hell with the consequences.

Finally, she stopped in front of him, clutching her small purse. Whatever words she might have said dissolved against her dry tongue as Caleb's gaze lingered on her legs and then slowly made its way up the snug fit of her dress until he finally looked into her eyes. Bryna jutted her chin out the tiniest bit and smiled suggestively, waiting for his thoughts, which she was sure he was about to share.

"Intriguing."

Bryna shivered. She'd never been referred to as intriguing before; she decided she liked it. More, she was determined to prove herself exactly that.

She asked in a voice she hardly recognized, "Shall we?"

The upward quirk of the corners of his mouth made her own water. "We most definitely shall.…"

4

CALEB HAD CERTAINLY KNOWN his share of women. And prided himself on being able to pigeonhole them within five minutes. Who they were. What they were after. How long their liaison would last.

But Bryna Metaxas was proving a charming enigma.

Throughout dinner she was by turns openly flirtatious and smartly businesslike depending on which way he slanted the conversation.

She even seemed to realize exactly what he was doing with each turn, a small, acknowledging smile letting him know that he wouldn't always get his way.

Little did she know that he always got exactly that, he reflected as he sipped his post-dinner coffee.

"So, tell me, Mr. Payne. Since it's obvious you didn't ask me here to discuss business matters—in fact, I'm certain you haven't even looked at the proposals I left at your office—then why did you ask?"

Direct. Fresh. Another woman might think the reason for his invitation unimportant, instead focusing on what she could gain from it. Not Bryna.

"Is it a sin to want to enjoy the company of a beautiful woman?"

She licked the side of her fork in a decidedly sexy manner that they both knew was done for reasons other than enjoyment of the slice of chocolate mousse torte she'd ordered for dessert.

"I should think you'd have at least a dozen beautiful women you could call."

Caleb leaned back in the leather booth, his suit pants feeling tight around the crotch at the sight of her tongue darting out of her red painted lips and drawing slowly along the silver. He could think of one place in particular where he'd like to see her do that, and the idea was so tempting it was more intoxicating than the snifter of cognac he'd ordered along with his coffee.

"I could also ask why you were free on a Friday evening." He hiked a brow. "Or did you cancel something?"

"You're redirecting the conversation. Again."

Caleb chuckled and narrowed his eyes as he considered her.

"Okay." He leaned forward, placing his hands on the table between them. "I recently found myself at the end of six-month relationship," he said. "And

hadn't thought about not having company this weekend. And, the truth is, I do not like to dine alone."

She appeared surprised that he'd offered up what
he had. She leaned forward, as well, their hands
nearly meeting on the table. "I appreciate the honesty,
but that still doesn't explain why you called me."

"I called you," he began, turning his hands palm
up, aware of the way they itched to touch her, her
cheek, her neck, her breasts.... "Because I was
reasonably sure that you wouldn't sleep with me
tonight."

That apparently surprised her as she sat back. But
she recovered quickly.

She didn't appear in any hurry to offer up a response. And he liked that. Indeed, he enjoyed watching her face as she turned his explanation over in
her beautiful head, her eyes growing dark, her smile
provocatively sexy.

He'd bet she was slowly rubbing her foot against
the calf of her other leg under the table.

"Reasonably?" she asked, her voice quiet and
loaded with suggestion.

Nice. "Mmm."

"Because?"

"Because you wouldn't want me to get the wrong
impression."

She smiled. "Ah, because of our business connection."

"There is no business connection."

"Yet."

He grinned. "Yet."

"So you think I'm above sleeping with someone for business gain," she said quietly, putting another forkful of torte in her mouth. A mouth that was driving him to absolute distraction.

"I think you're very much above it."

"And if I invited you back to my place?"

"I'd have to insist we go to mine.…"

OKAY, SO HE'D CALLED her bluff.

And Bryna practically shivered from head to toe at the thought of going through with it.

It had been sweet torture sitting across from him, wanting to know more, but unable to find the words with which to ask him.

Oh, they'd talked. But she'd been too distracted by the line of his jaw…the strength of his hands…the length of his fingers…the sureness of his dark gaze to challenge him to a verbal rather than visual duel.

And now she had the chance at a physical contest…

The heat of his hand where it rested on her arm as they walked toward the restaurant door seared her bare flesh.

At the curb, a limo instantly pulled up and the driver came out to open the door for them.

If she got into that car, she knew she'd be a goner. She would be unable to stop herself from going as far as he intended to take this. And while an elemental, wild side of her was all for it, her mind cried out that it was too fast, too soon. To sleep with him would be placing the advantage in his court and swipe all the balls from hers.

Instead of entering the car, she turned toward him, finding him so close that her thigh ended up pressing against a certain, nicely rock-hard part of him. She shivered and looked up into his eyes, her hand resting against his chest.

"As tempting as the invitation is," she whispered, her breath grazing the jaw she'd been wanted to taste all night, "I'm afraid you're right. There's no chance I'm going to sleep with you tonight."

He smelled of limes and one hundred percent hot male.

She watched the corners of his mouth turn up. "Shame," he said, his fingers brushing against her hips and then resting there, pulling her imperceptibly closer to him, crowding her against his arousal.

"Mmm," she agreed, her heart pounding a loud rhythm in her chest.

She leaned in as if to kiss him, her gaze moving from his eyes to his mouth and back again.

She stepped back instead and waved for a taxi.

"Thank you for dinner," she murmured.

"Thank you for the company."

"Anytime."

His eyes sparkled dangerously. "I might just take you up on that offer."

She hoped he did.

So soft…so warm…

Her body throbbed with yearning, wet, needy. She arched her back, reaching for Caleb as he leaned above her. But he always seemed just out of reach, smiling that knowing, wicked grin.…

Her own moan woke her up.

Bryna rose quickly to her elbows and pushed back the tangle of hair in her eyes. She blinked her old bedroom at the Metaxas estate into view. White-curtained canopy. Pink-and-white wallpaper. A white marble fireplace. Stuffed animals stacked up in one corner.

She blew out a long breath. It had been two days since she'd said goodbye to Caleb at the restaurant, and ever since he'd haunted her dreams. Always there, always just within reach, yet outside it.

Bryna whipped the covers back and maneuvered her bare legs over the side of the bed, paying little mind that her simple cotton nightgown was bunched up around her thighs. She reached for her cell on the nightstand and clicked it open. No calls. No texts. She closed it again and put it back down and then padded across the large room toward the connecting bathroom.

Friday night it had taken all of her will after getting into that cab not to direct the driver to turn around and follow the limo instead. The reaction had surprised her. She'd never met a man who'd gotten under her skin to such a mind-robbing degree. She wanted to feel his hands on her. Wanted to put her mouth on him. Wanted to spend the night exploring the seeds of sensation their dinner together had planted in her. So much so that to prevent herself from pursuing him the next day, she'd driven back to Earnest for the night when usually she drove up Sunday morning for family brunch.

Within twenty minutes Bryna was showered and dressed in a white slacks and a purple short-sleeved blouse, no less bothered than she'd been when she'd awakened. But determined to shake off the peculiar feelings any which way she could.

She slid into her sandals and went downstairs. It was nine and brunch wasn't until ten-thirty, but she wasn't surprised when she found her uncle Percy and Troy already up and on the back deck enjoying coffee.

"Good morning." She kissed her uncle on the check and squeezed her cousin's shoulder as she passed on the way to the chair next to him.

"Well, good morning to you, too," Percy said, folding the business section of the paper and placing it on the table. "Nice to see you here so early."

"I actually came in last night," she said, pouring herself a cup of coffee.

"Oh? Any particular reason for that?"

Just that she couldn't seem to get a maddening man out of her mind, that's all. "No. Just decided I'd like to wake up at home this morning, that's all."

And the grand ol' estate was that, wasn't it? All

800 acres of land and 25,000 square feet of house. Plenty of room for them all to reside without living on top of each other.

Home. It was odd, sometimes, to think that for her it had once been a simpler place just outside Seattle. The past twelve years since her parents' deaths, this had been where her old grade cards, school photographs and swim meet medals were stored. This sweeping mansion that sat on a hill overlooking the town of Earnest. And no matter how much she claimed independence, this was where she went when she needed to find peace. When she needed to touch base with her foundation.

And it was her uncle Percy and cousins Troy and Ari who were her immediate family. They were always there for her.

"Have you added enough sugar?" Troy asked now.

Bryna looked at where she was stirring in yet another teaspoonful. She frowned and took a sip, making a face.

"Uh-oh. Looks like man troubles to me."

They all turned as the more outspoken of them had stepped out onto the deck.

Ari.

Bryna smiled and then grimaced. "Correct me if I'm wrong, but you usually have to have a man in order for there to be any kind of trouble, don't you?"

"Not necessarily." Ari reached over her and

plucked a grape from a bunch on a tray. "Trouble enters when you want a man you can't have."

Troy rustled his section of the *Seattle Times*. "Look who's the expert suddenly."

Bryna looked behind Ari. Could it be he'd come to the brunch alone this week? She knew a spot of hope.

Then Elena came outside, apologizing for her delay. "I'm not even showing yet, but I swear my bladder is the size of a pea."

Bryna frowned as she watched the other woman greet her uncle the same way she had and then say good morning to Troy, who actually grinned at her.

Where was the animosity? The anger?

Oh, well. It looked as if the job would have to fall to her. When the other woman took the chair next to her, Bryna focused solely on her coffee.

Even she admitted to being surprised at her reaction to her cousin's intended…especially since Elena was pregnant with what they all hoped would be the first of the next Metaxas generation. But so much had been riding on that deal with Philippidis. To just throw it all away because of a woman was unthinkable to her.

She frowned. If only Elena would have kept her legs closed, and her hand on her ex-groom's arm, right now the first production line would be running and the second would be under construction, employing at least two hundred of the town's hurting residents.

The thought made her mind drift back to Caleb and her own conflicted feelings for him.

Of course, the difference lay in that she wasn't engaged to marry someone else so no one would be hurt if things spiraled out of control and then went south.

She swallowed hard.

Other than herself, that is....

5

WAS IT TIME YET?

Caleb looked at his watch as the presentation dragged on. There were ten men in the room for the weekly Wednesday meeting that had been scheduled for that morning, then delayed until afternoon because Manolis Philippidis was late flying in.

He glanced at the modern-day Greek tycoon at the end of the table. Manolis held a small coffee cup in his meaty fingers, his dark eyes on the acquisitions head who was talking about the pros and cons of buying a small business out of Minnesota that made public buses that ran on natural gas.

The new business was green business.

He looked at his watch again.

"Are we keeping you from something, Caleb?" Manolis asked, interrupting the speaker.

He sat back, grinning easily. "No. Not at all."

"Perhaps we're boring you, then?"

Caleb's smile grew tight.

It was well-known that there was no love lost between the two men. Which was why Caleb had never worked directly for him. Would never hand that kind of power to a man who would just as soon fire you as look at you.

No. Caleb liked that he was a well-paid consultant to the company. A very well-paid consultant. Which sometimes required him to sit through trying meetings that had nothing to do with him. And suffer a man who was otherwise insufferable.

"To the contrary. I was thinking about the three other more viable gas-powered bus ventures that are looking for investors rather than to be bought outright." He raised a brow. "Would you like me to continue? Or shall we get back to the meeting agenda?"

As expected, Manolis glowered at him, finished off his coffee and then looked at his own watch. "I believe this meeting is concluded."

If there was one man who hated wasting time as much as Caleb it was Philippidis.

The Greek stood and everyone else at the table hurried to do the same. All but for Caleb, who took his time getting to his feet.

He extended his hand toward Manolis, who shook it. "You have information on these other companies?"

"I sent proposals to the ventures head a month ago."

Manolis nodded. "Let him know I want to hear more about them at next month's meeting."

"Very well."

The other man straightened his tailor-made suit jacket as if having just made an important decision and muttered his goodbyes before leaving the room.

Caleb followed him out, heading directly for his own office.

"Has…" he began as he neared Nancy's desk.

She interrupted. "Miss Metaxas is waiting in your office, as you directed, sir."

The sun had just emerged from the heavy gray clouds.

BRYNA READ THE SPINES of the books in the cases that lined Caleb's office. Business tomes were interspaced with leather-bound classic fiction novels and philosophy titles. She wondered if he'd read them or if they'd come by way of a professional decorator. He was, after all, a consultant with the Philippidis company, meaning this wasn't his permanent office, but rather a temporary one.

But how temporary? How many years had he been working with him?

She moved down the bookcase, squinting to read the script on a recognition-of-excellence plaque that had been propped against the books.

She looked around. There were no photographs, personal or professional. It seemed to her that everything was purposely displayed to reveal very little about the office's inhabitant beyond his power and success.

She'd moved to where she could see behind his desk and now looked over her shoulder, eyeing the drawers there.

The door opened and she jumped.

Caleb seemed to take in the situation in one glance. He slowly closed the door even as Bryna walked to the visitor's side of the desk.

"Nice to see you again, Miss Metaxas," he said in that low, deep way he had of speaking.

She cleared her throat. "The pleasure's all mine, Mr. Payne."

He stood looking at her for a moment, not long, but long enough to encourage that longing to wend through her veins anew.

"We'll see," he said, but whether it was a threat or a promise, she didn't know.

He walked toward his chair.

Did he know what effect he had on her? She'd offer an unqualified yes. He gave the impression of being a man who was aware of everyone and everything in any room he inhabited. And likely commanded the gazes of every female within a half-mile radius, along with a majority of men if just from sheer envy.

"I was pleased when you called for this appointment," she said. "Would you like to go over the proposals?"

He opened the right desk drawer, watching her face as he did so. "Only one of them has possibilities."

"Oh? Which?"

"The second."

She smiled.

"That's the one you intended me to choose."

"It's the one I'd hoped you'd choose."

Of the three, the proposal was the most solid and followed the basic tenets of the original, only scaled down. Instead of four production lines, they'd begin with one. Rather than go whole hog, she proposed starting with a limited offering. Troy's plans were large, ambitious, much like her cousin himself. But as she'd tried without success to explain to him, perhaps it was better to start small with the potential to grow than big with the possibility of failure…if he succeeded in selling the grand idea at all.…

Caleb walked to a polished table near the window that held four chairs. He put the proposal in question down. "There are a number of things we need to reconfigure."

Bryna followed him and pulled out the chair next to the one he stood behind. But he didn't sit. Instead, he shrugged out of his jacket, hung it on a hanger inside a door that she suspected led to a full bathroom, and then undid his cufflinks, sliding them into his pockets before rolling up his sleeves.

Her mouth went dry. Even though he was going for comfort, he still looked more elegant than any man she'd ever seen. And that was saying something because her cousins weren't exactly slouches when it came to the man department.

He'd begun talking, presumably about the proposal, but Bryna couldn't make a word out. Her ears had stopped accepting input as her heart rate sped up. She was too caught up watching him take off his tie and undo his top three buttons. His waist was narrow where his Egyptian broadcloth shirt was tucked into his slacks, the belt further emphasizing the difference from his wide chest and shoulders.

"Is something the matter, Miss Metaxas?" he asked, leaning a large-palmed hand on the table on the other side of her.

The pungent scent of limes assaulted her senses, and his sudden nearness made her lick her parched lips.

"Bryna…please," she said, sounding more in control than she felt.

Dear Lord, how did any woman manage to conduct official business with this man?

She gathered her wits about her and smiled up at him. "I thought we moved beyond formalities the other night."

A hint of a grin. A shadow of stubble.

He was ten, maybe twelve inches from her. So easy to lean in and run the tip of her tongue along his jawline…

He stood suddenly. "You're right. It's late. Perhaps we should reschedule this meeting."

Bryna's eyes widened. "No." She forced herself to

focus on the notepad she'd laid on the table before her. "I'm fine. Sorry. It's been a long day. I just drove in from Earnest after putting a full day in…"

He grasped her chair back.

Bryna silently cursed herself. Had she just put the kibosh on a business deal because she couldn't control her runaway hormones?

So she'd spent the past six days imagining the many ways Caleb Payne knew to please a woman. And had explored a couple of those ways with her own hands. She could separate business from pleasure.

"Very well. I'll have my secretary call yours to reschedule," she said.

He pushed her chair back in after she rose to her feet.

"I'm afraid you misunderstood me, Miss…Bryna. I'm not ending this meeting. I'm merely suggesting we move it."

To your bed? her mind offered. "Oh?" she fairly croaked.

"To a restaurant. Preferably one that offers up a good pinot noir."

Relief flushed her system. "Ah. How much of this has to do with your not liking to eat alone?"

"Nothing. I merely see an opportunity for us to kill two birds with one proverbial stone."

Was it her, or had he just leaned in closer to her? Limes.

He'd definitely moved nearer.

Her mouth watered.

"I know just the place...." she offered.

SO IT WAS AGREED. They would split up. She would go home to freshen up and he would pick her up at her place in an hour.

Bryna tried not to run down the hall outside his office in her hurry to lessen the time between now and when they'd meet again.

God, when was the last time she'd felt this kind of charged anticipation? It had been so long ago she couldn't remember. She could scold herself for acting unprofessionally later. Right now she was enjoying the zing of awareness, the hungry longing between her thighs, the rasp of her nipples against her bra as she walked.

"Oh!"

She ran headlong into someone coming around the corner to the elevators.

"Pardon me. I wasn't watching where I was going," she said automatically.

Then she brought the man into focus and all apology left her.

Manolis Philippidis.

Stupid, stupid, stupid.

This was his company. She should have taken into consideration that the chances of running into him here would be greater than average.

Still, she was unprepared for facing the man

responsible for so much of the trouble her family's company was in.

His face registered nothing and then it seemed to dawn on him who she was. They'd met more than a few times at the mill offices and he'd tried to pick her up at least once.

The guy gave her the creeps despite his Greek Sean Connery good looks.

"Miss Metaxas, isn't it?" he asked, looking behind her as if to see who she was with.

"Mr. Philippidis. Hello."

"It's nice to see you."

His eyes told her it was anything but.

She realized that the hand he'd put on her sleeve to steady her was still there, now caressing her.

She shuddered.

"Are you here alone?"

"Yes. Yes, I am."

"Well, then. Why don't we go into my office where we can…catch up."

The last thing she wanted was to catch up with Manolis Philippidis. She'd intended to put this deal together without having anything to do with him, in essence employing Caleb's services as a consultant to help her to attract investors.

"I'm sorry," she said, "but I'm late for an appointment. Maybe another…"

His hand tightened on her arm. "I insist."

She stared at him. He wasn't insinuating that he'd physically take her to his office, was he? He'd better be careful or she'd have to use some of her Tae Bo moves on him.

"Miss Metaxas came for a meeting with me."

Caleb.

Bryna instantly relaxed as he came to stand next to her, his tie tightened, his jacket back on.

She watched as the two men indulged in one of those stare-off things that she sometimes saw Troy and Ari do even as she discreetly shrugged off Philippidis's hand.

"Oh? And why wasn't I apprised of the situation?" Manolis asked.

Caleb's smile was just shy of threatening. "There's nothing to apprise you of."

"If you'll excuse me," Bryna said quietly. "I really must go."

Her gaze flitted to Caleb's face.

"I don't want to be late for that meeting."

She moved around them.

"It was…nice to see you again, Mr. Philippidis."

She couldn't have hurried for the elevators faster had she dived for them, and was relieved when the doors closed, blocking out the two men staring after her.

Cripes.

6

FROM HERE ON HE AND BRYNA were going to meet outside Philippidis's offices.

Damn. Why hadn't he thought that the Greek might bump into her?

Why hadn't he considered what his reaction to seeing the old man's hands on her might be?

He and the wealthy businessman were already a drop of bad blood away from parting professional company altogether, no matter the consequences to his own business ambitions. But he didn't want it to be over a woman. No matter how tantalizing.

Even though he'd spent a great deal of his career acting as the Greek's wingman, facilitating deals that would have otherwise fallen through without some careful finessing, he'd always remained independent, working solely on contract, never directly for him. The professional relationship had fattened his accounts and allowed him room to spearhead his own deals. As far as everyone was concerned, the only person he was loyal to was himself and the deal.

Which was likely why Bryna Metaxas had sought him out; if she'd thought for a minute that he might screw her over out of allegiance to Philippidis, then he would have been the last person she'd approach.

"Sir?"

He blinked at the driver who spoke to him over the intercom in the back of his limo.

"Would you like me to ring for the lady?"

They were at Bryna's apartment already.

Caleb scratched his face. He'd meant to shave before leaving the office but had been too preoccupied to do more than return a couple of urgent phone calls. He looked through the window to find Bryna already coming through the lobby doors.

Some of the tension coiled in his muscles loosened. A woman with no pretenses. Who was ready when she said she'd be and didn't make him wait.

Refreshing.

The driver immediately got out and opened the door for her and she slipped in.

Despite the daytime summer heat, the night was cool. She wore a light white pashmina over her dark fuchsia dress.

"I'm sorry if I made you wait," she said.

Caleb relaxed farther into the rich leather seat, enjoying the view of her. The deep V of the sleeveless sheath. The length of her smooth legs. "Not at all."

The driver got back behind the wheel. "Sir?" he asked over the intercom.

Caleb held Bryna's gaze. "I'd like to suggest some-place different if you don't mind?"

"Sure. Whatever you like."

He grinned. "Dangerous comment, that."

Her chin came up a fraction of an inch, telling him that she stood by her words.

Whatever he liked…

An intriguing prospect, indeed.

He reached up and pressed the intercom button. "Home, James."

THE LAST THING on Bryna's mind was the proposal. Or food, for that matter. From the moment she slid in-side Caleb's limo, she'd felt as if she was in a cocoon, a cottony blanket that muted sounds, but somehow made colors more vibrant. And heightened her sexual awareness of the man who'd played the lead role in many a dream as of late.

His penthouse apartment was as impersonal as his office had been, but no less sumptuous. A wall of windows overlooked the Seattle skyline, the view mesmerizing her as the glowing orange ball of the sun sank behind the Space Needle. The main room was combination sitting and dining area, with a rounded corner of glass devoted to what could be called an entertainment area. There was a top-of-the-line stereo system that was revealed behind an etched panel as Caleb switched on an instrumental jazz CD, filling the large room with the sound of a smoky sax from multiple unseen speakers.

A man that knew what he liked, and liked what he knew.

She ran her hand over a gleaming black grand piano, tinkling a few of the keys.

"Do you play?"

He poured them two glasses of wine at a nearby antique liquor cabinet. "I play."

She rounded the piano. "I'd like to see that."

He held out a glass and she accepted it. "It's generally something I do in private."

"Why am I not surprised?"

He cocked his head slightly.

"I'm guessing you don't let many people see you with your guard down. And…" She touched a key again. "Music takes passion."

His eyes glimmered darkly. "Plenty of…people have seen my passion."

"I bet." She smiled into her wineglass. The smooth, bloodred liquid flowed lightly over her tongue, leaving just the faintest essence of lavender. "I'm not talking about sex, Caleb." The moment the *s* word was out of her mouth, her entire body reacted to the prospect of having some of it with him now, tonight. "I have no doubt that you're very, very good at that." She cleared her crowded throat. "You're probably very, very good at everything you do."

An image of his mouth leaning in to claim hers made her lips tingle.

"I'm talking about doing something that bares you to someone else, from which you have nothing to gain."

He paused, weighing her words, obviously intrigued. "I've played some in front of groups. However small."

"Mmm. That's performing. Not revealing."

He followed her path around the piano, running his finger over the keys much as she had, but the sounds he elicited were much more pleasing than her unskilled pokes. "Perhaps."

She shivered, the one, quiet word traveling like a sigh over her skin.

"And perhaps there are some things that I like to claim for myself alone."

He'd stepped up behind her, and his last couple of words exited as warm breath against her bare shoulder.

"However briefly," she whispered.

"Meaning?"

He moved his head to hover over her other shoulder, making her hyperaware of his nearness, his intentions.

"Meaning that you can play the piano as long as you want…and then you can leave it to sit without paying it another thought until the desire moves you to play again."

He was silent for a long moment and then he made a small humming sound. "You smell good."

She moved her head to the side, giving him access

to her neck if he so chose to take advantage of it. "Thank you."

"So, Miss Metaxas, are you suggesting that I might treat people the same way as I treat my piano?"

She lifted her wineglass to her lips, her fingers trembling ever so slightly. "From what I've seen of you so far, I'm guessing that you're a man of strict control."

She felt his lips against her shoulder. A shiver shimmered through her, followed by a flash of heat.

She turned almost abruptly and smiled up at him. "I bet you make love the same way you conduct business—with methodical thoroughness."

He held her gaze. "Would you like to put that theory to the test?"

She leaned in until their lips were the width of a butterfly wing away. "I'd like to see you lose control."

His dark right brow rose slightly.

She'd surprised him. And knowing that turned her on all the more.

She ran her tongue along her bottom lip and then breathed a light kiss on him.

Caleb reached toward a square panel in the wall to his left and pushed a button.

"Sir?" a male voice immediately responded.

"Lionel, put dinner in the warmer. I'll see you in the morning."

"Very good, sir. Good evening."

"THE WINDOWS CONTINUE in here..."

Caleb stood in the open doorway of his master bedroom, absorbing Bryna's soft silhouette against the golden, waning light. He didn't paint, but if he did, he thought it would be this image, this moment he'd like to commit eternally to canvas.

She moved her head to the side. "As does the music..."

He couldn't remember the last time a woman had found her way to his bedroom so quickly. Last week's impromptu dinner aside, they hadn't even dated. And even this evening, the plan had been to continue the meeting that had begun in his office.

Her proposal was long forgotten in his briefcase by the front door.

He watched as she reached behind her, slowly unzipping her dress.

"I figure—" her voice was soft and low "—that we're both adults. Whatever this is...this thing that's crackling between us...it need not interfere with our business dealings...."

She turned, allowing the dress to fall in a puddle to the ground, revealing that she wore absolutely nothing underneath. No lacy bra. No expensive underwear. It was just Bryna and a simple gold necklace bearing a small cross and her high-heeled sandals.

His brow moved upward again at the thought that she'd been bare-bottomed since the moment she slid into his limo.

There was no game playing with her. No angles to work or rules to obey.

And his throbbing hard-on told him that her naked honesty appealed to him on several levels.

He placed his wineglass on the credenza next to where she'd left hers and crossed the room, coming to stand directly in front of her. She looked up into his face, her expression needy and challenging all at once.

Caleb took her in, inch by tantalizing inch.

Her breasts were small and pert, untouched by a plastic surgeon's knife. Dark nipples puckered, as thick as the tip of his pinky finger. Her waist was narrow and her hips flared…her womanhood neatly trimmed but left natural.

He'd taken his jacket off in the other room, but now he systematically loosened and then took off his tie and began unbuttoning his shirt. It joined her dress on the floor along with his slacks and within moments he stood facing her, as naked as she was.

And feeling oddly emotionally bare.

He leaned in at the same time she did and they kissed. She tasted sweet as he slid his tongue against hers, desire mingling with the fine wine.

She murmured something he couldn't make out and then she was swaying into him, her nipples grazing his chest, her hips against his. His hard-on throbbed against her soft belly and her musky, female scent filled his senses.

Caleb recalled thinking that he'd like to be surprised by a woman for a change.

He believed he just had been....

7

BRYNA'S ENTIRE BODY trembled, tautened, waiting for her to exhale.

Everything about Caleb Payne was long and lean. And his expression was so intense that she couldn't look anywhere but into his mesmerizing eyes.

She'd never bought into the vampire myth. But if she had, she would have suspected he was one.

He lifted a hand to her shoulder and slid it up over her collarbone, then her neck, threading his fingers into the hair at the nape of her neck. He tilted her head back and then kissed her so thoroughly her knees nearly gave out from under her.

She'd known he would be good. There had never been any question that he would see to her every need even as he quenched his own. But it was one thing to anticipate something, quite another to experience it.

Her heart thudded so erratically in her chest that

she was concerned she wouldn't survive her reaction to him. Her lungs would accept nothing but shallow intakes of air. Her body was on fire, seeming to seek a fundamental meeting with or without her cooperation as she pressed her hips harder against his, the crisp hair on his thighs rasping against her smoother skin.

Before she'd realized he'd moved, she felt his fingers against her bottom. Bryna shifted her feet, giving him better access. The instant his fingertip touched her swollen folds, she nearly collapsed altogether, the sensation swirling with the anticipation.

He supported her weight against him, his index finger dipping into her saturated channel and using her own fluid to lubricate the attention he focused on her aching core.

Bryna grasped his shoulders and threw her head back.

She heard his groan and then he was sweeping her up into his arms and carrying her to the mammoth bed across the room. He carefully laid her down against the white comforter, but didn't immediately follow. Instead, he collected a box from a nightstand drawer and tossed it to the bed beside her. She reached for the condoms, then forgot them altogether when he spread her knees with his, standing above her next to the bed.

Bryna restlessly licked her lips, allowing her gaze to move over his magnificent form. His penis was stiff and thick, the head nearly hitting his navel. She swallowed hard, filled with the need to press her tongue against the turgid flesh.

But Caleb had something else in mind as he slid his hands up her legs to her inner thighs.

She automatically opened to him, spreading her legs and bending her ankles. He leaned in and she surrendered her ability to breathe altogether as he parted her folds and pressed his tongue against her tight bud.

Bryna twisted her fists into the bedding, holding on for dear life as her hips bucked involuntarily. Caleb flattened a palm against her trembling stomach, holding her still even as his other hand caressed and tugged and stroked her, his mouth hot and knowing.

This couldn't be real. She had to be dreaming. Sex was never this good. The earth stopped spinning and she hovered somewhere between this world and an alternate universe. A place where everything was white and sweet and so very, very exquisite. One didn't need food or water in order to survive, only this…this incredible facet of being.

He slid a finger inside her dripping opening, stroking her with a touch so skillful that she burst into yet another realm, this one red and gold and hot…so very hot. She reached for him, wanting, needing, to feel him inside her, now.

She'd never known such a complete urgency. Inhibition and thought were left far behind. There existed only a greedy desire to claim him.

He granted her wish and lifted to kiss her. She tasted her musk on his tongue as she slid her head one way, then the next, wanting to swallow him whole even as she reached for his erection. Her fingers curved around the hard flesh, barely meeting around his thick width. She guided him to her sex and bore upward against him.

He slowly slid in to the hilt.

Everything halted. Bryna's gasp emerged silent; her heart contracted and then stopped. They were no longer two separate entities but one, joined, together.

Then her heart beat again, her gasp echoed through the air and time started back up in a sort of slow motion animation.

At some point, Caleb withdrew and finally sheathed himself.

Finally she could no longer take the chaos building inside her and Bryna surrendered to what easily rated as the best orgasm of her life.

LONG HOURS LATER, Caleb watched Bryna unabashedly coax a bit of lobster meat from a stubborn claw with her tongue, the sucking sound making his manhood stiffen all over again.

It was a source of amusement and consternation that he seemed to be in a highly aroused state whenever he was near her.

"Which restaurant did you say this was from?" she asked, licking her fingers.

They were sitting at the butcher-block island in his penthouse kitchen on two stools, a single candle lighting the room, her wearing his white shirt, two buttons strategically holding the material together, while he wore a pair of black silk drawstring pants. At somewhere around one, after hearing her stomach growl, he'd suggested they finally see to that dinner they'd intended to have earlier.

That meant they'd indulged in five straight hours of mind-blowing sex.

And he wanted more....

He told her the name of the restaurant and she nodded, although he suspected she hadn't truly heard him. She was openly gazing at his abs and then down lower to where his hard-on tented the material of his pants. Her pupils were large in her green eyes, her hair a tangled mass around her head. He'd never seen anything so sexy in his life. She hadn't dived for the shower before coming into the kitchen like other women he'd known. Hadn't stopped to reapply makeup or squirt perfume. She looked wondrously natural and open and well sexed, her scent—their combined scent—teasing his senses.

How long had it been since he'd felt, truly felt, a woman around him? When he hadn't pulled on a condom before entering? He wasn't sure what had compelled him not to do it now. But he'd been filled with an urgent need to sample her, unimpeded.

He'd wanted to feel her. Pure and simple.

She picked up her wineglass with sticky fingers

and nearly dropped it. Laughing, she took a sip, considering him over the rim.

"You've barely touched a thing," she murmured.

That's because all he could think about was hauling her back on top of him. Right now. Where he sat on the stool.

"I had a big lunch."

The corners of her mouth turned up. "So did I. But I'm still ravenous."

"I noticed."

Her chewing slowed and she began to put the claw down.

"No, no. Please don't alter your behavior because of me. I'm enjoying watching you eat."

And he was. She did it with such childlike enthusiasm that he was fascinated. She used the back of her wrist to push her hair back, baring the perfect oval of her face to his gaze. Her lips were slightly swollen, her color high. And she couldn't have been more beautiful to him.

She looked around the kitchen. "Nice place. Own or rent?"

"Own."

"Are you from Seattle?"

He shook his head. "New England."

"I thought I detected a bit of an accent."

"Oh?"

"Yeah. Sexy. JFKish somehow. But more subtle."

"Thank you. I think."

Her soft laugh did something odd to his stomach. "You're welcome." She wiped her hands on the linen napkin and picked up a fresh roll. "So…are you planning to stay here? In Seattle, I mean?"

He lifted a brow. Funny, but no one had actually asked him that before. Perhaps they just assumed that he would. Or maybe they weren't interested one way or the other.

"Depends on what the future brings."

She nodded. "Businesswise."

"Yes."

She chewed thoughtfully. "I've lived here all my life. Well, here and in Earnest. After my parents…"

Her sentence abruptly ended and she grimaced.

"After your parents…" he prompted.

She put the roll down and sipped from her wineglass. "After my parents died."

Silence reigned for a few moments.

She cleared her throat. "Sorry. I usually don't share things of that nature on a first date. I hate when people offer up their life stories." She made a face. "Poor me. My parents died in a plane crash when I was twelve and I had to go live with my uncle and cousins in Earnest." She drank again. "Talk about darkening the mood."

"So this is our first date, then?"

She looked at him without saying anything. Then, "I don't know. Isn't it? Or is it a booty call?"

"Booty call?"

She laughed. "Yes. You know. I'm not doing

anything. You're not doing anything. Why don't we get together and do nothing together."

He shifted on the stool. "I prefer date."

Another laugh. "So do I."

"Do you indulge in a lot of…"

"Booty calls?"

He coughed midway through taking a sip of wine. "Yes."

"This would be my first. You know, if we were classifying it as such."

"But we're not."

"No." Her smile was dazzling. "So I guess that means I've never…indulged in one." She forked a roasted potato and stuck it into her mouth, watching him closely. After finally swallowing, she said, "And in case you're wondering, no, I don't usually sleep with men on first dates, either. They're lucky if they get a kiss."

He hadn't been wondering, but he liked that she'd shared the information. "Then they would be lucky, indeed."

To his delight, she blushed.

He sat back. A woman who had blatantly invited his touch, yet blushed afterward at his mention of it. Intriguing…

"You know, you really should eat something or else I'm going to have to stop."

The chuckle that erupted from him was unexpected and sounded foreign to his own ears. He picked up his fork, speared some lobster meat and then raised it for her consideration. "Happy?"

He put it in his mouth.

She smiled around her potato. "I will be when you swallow."

He did just that. "You couldn't possibly have expected me to spit it out?"

She shrugged. "You never know. You come across some strange people."

He could attest to that. He'd dated a model who would eat nearly everything on the table, including from his and others' plates, and then disappear into the ladies' room, before returning and ordering dessert.

He'd given her the benefit of the doubt…until he'd caught her in the act at his apartment. He'd heard sounds that concerned him, knocked on the door and then opened it to find her crouched before the toilet.

She'd smiled, brushed her teeth and then rejoined him in the living room as if nothing had happened.

But something had. And he'd summarily dismissed her, suggesting she seek out help.

"There was this one guy I went out with who had to trade texts with his mother every five minutes. It would have been okay if he was fifteen, but he was in his thirties." She shook her head. "But that's another taboo topic for me on first dates."

"What is?"

"Having the 'loves that have come before'

discussion. Or, worse, 'those by whom I've been spurned.'"

"And this guy…was he…"

"Oh, God, no. The first date was the last. And if I'm not mistaken, I believe I feigned stomach cramps halfway through the meal."

She picked up another lobster claw and squinted at him. "Seems I'm doing all the talking here. And, again, you're not eating."

That's because Caleb was riveted to the way she fit her lips just so over the red claw.

She caught on to his preoccupation, put the claw down and cleaned up before taking a long sip of wine.

"Shall we move on to dessert?" she asked, snaking a hand around his neck and pulling him in for a kiss unlike any that had come before.…

8

CALEB SAT IN HIS OFFICE staring out the windows at downtown Seattle. Though two days had passed since Bryna had stayed the night at his place, he couldn't help revisiting the evening. Remembering the sexy curve of her hip. The sensitivity of the back of her knees. Her soft cries when she'd reached orgasm… again and again.

He'd awakened the following morning with an ache for her the size of Washington State. He'd reached for her across the bed, only to discover she'd gone. No note. No promise of more. No word on whether she'd be back.

He'd finally given in and called her cell phone yesterday morning, but she hadn't picked up. And he hadn't left a message.

"Caleb?"

"Hmm?" He turned from the window and looked

at where Philippidis staff directly accountable to him were wrapping up the morning meeting.

"Anything you'd like to add?"

He straightened in his chair. "No."

"Okay, then," Jason Hasselbeck said. "Then we'll meet again Wednesday morning."

The participants began to disperse, but Caleb asked Hasselbeck to stay behind.

After the last staff member left the room, Caleb took Bryna's proposal from his desk drawer. "I want you to take a look at this for me. Let me know what you think."

Hasselbeck's brows rose as he browsed the first page, but he didn't say anything. Obviously he'd seen the Metaxas name. And if there was one thing Philippidis had accomplished, it was to have anything associated with Ari Metaxas banned from the building... unless it was to help him in his plan for revenge.

Caleb rose to his feet, waiting until Hasselbeck looked at him full in the face. "I don't think I have to tell you that this is to remain between you and me."

Although Caleb had hired Jason, he was ultimately Philippidis's employee, so he knew what he was asking of him was borderline, but he wanted his opinion.

"Are you seriously considering trying to resell him on a company that he's turned on?"

They both knew that the chances of that happening lay somewhere between nil and zero.

"If we can make the numbers work, maybe."

"And if we can't?"

Caleb sat back down in his chair. "We'll cross that bridge when we come to it. This is merely a preliminary look. Nothing official has been offered or agreed to."

Hasselbeck looked suspicious. And he had every right to. Caleb hadn't hired him because he was stupid. He knew that Caleb didn't take anything on, even preliminarily, unless there was a very strong chance he would proceed with it.

He also likely suspected that Caleb had every intention of shopping it around if he couldn't sell Philippidis on the deal.

Hasselbeck left the office and Caleb sat for a long time staring at his empty desktop. He had plenty to do, but he didn't feel particularly interested in pursuing any of the ten other projects waiting for him to okay the next step.

His intercom buzzed. "Sir, Mr. Palmer DeVoe is here to see you."

If anything were capable of nudging him from his current preoccupation, it was his old friend and ally. He told Nancy to send him in and then rose to his feet, buttoning his jacket as he rounded the desk.

The door opened.

"Well, look what the wind just blew in," he said, shaking Palmer's hand and then giving him a rare man hug.

There were few people he respected, either male or female, but Palmer DeVoe was one of them. A renowned business attorney, he worked for some of the most powerful companies out of Boston, starting with nothing but a law degree when he was in his twenties, and building his reputation until he was at the top of the letterhead of a very successful and lucrative law firm.

Caleb had acted on Palmer's behalf many times over the past ten years, usually in the role of aggressor, leveraging competing businesses that didn't want to budge, claiming properties that owners didn't want to sell. Essentially doing the dirty work so Palmer could keep his hands clean. And being well-rewarded for the part.

But it was more than business that bound them. Caleb had never been one for close friends of either sex, but when he and Palmer had found themselves essentially stranded in a small Texas town during the course of their first job together ten years ago—a flash flood had made it impossible for them to get out—they'd gone to the school gym to work out their restlessness on the basketball court…a tradition they continued over the years whenever their paths crossed.

Palmer seemed to know instinctively when to press for more information and when to let a topic lie. Especially when it came to items of a personal nature. And Caleb liked to the think he employed the same tact. And that had allowed a friendship to develop in addition to their professional association.

"I was in the neighborhood and thought I'd stop

by," Palmer said, the same affection that Caleb felt evident in his eyes.

"Bullshit. You're never in the neighborhood, and you never just drop in on anyone."

Was it him, or did Palmer look uncomfortable?

"Correct me if I'm wrong, but wasn't it you who said you weren't interested in losing the two business days it would take to fly halfway across the country to the Pacific NW and back?"

"Yeah, well…"

Another thought occurred to Caleb. One that was easy to forget because he'd only known Palmer in Boston. "Aren't you actually from the area around here somewhere?"

"Yes. A small town south of here."

Caleb raised his brows. "And you've never been back?"

"Not in fifteen years."

Caleb could understand wanting to escape the past. It was why he, himself, rarely returned to his old stomping grounds unless it was absolutely necessary. Even then, it was usually an in-and-out affair.

"Longing for old times?" he asked.

Palmer chuckled. "Not exactly." He looked around the office. "You got time to shoot a few hoops?"

Caleb grinned. "No. But I'll make time. It's been a while since I've enjoyed a little competition on the court.…"

He pushed the intercom for his secretary. "Nancy,

cancel all my appointments for this afternoon. Direct anything urgent to my cell phone."

BRYNA TYPED OUT a report on her laptop at her desk at Metaxas Limited, one eye on the door in case one of her cousins happened by and wanted to know what she was up to. She had an in-box full of menial tasks, but she was busy coming up with counterarguments to what she believed would be Caleb's arguments.

She smiled to herself as she typed up why her numbers should be accepted as was, or perhaps even be adjusted upward rather than down. She hadn't anticipated that having a potential partner would help bolster her confidence.

Potential partner...

Her fingers tripped over the keys. She grimaced and backtracked to delete the line of gibberish. Of course she meant "business" partner. To even consider getting involved with Caleb Payne was only asking for...well, a lot of pain.

She knew guys like him.

Okay, maybe she didn't know them, know them, but she was familiar with them. And was certainly familiar with his mode of operation. Date lady. Be seen dining and out and about with her. And just when others began to memorize her name, drop her cold.

Her research on him had shown he'd never been married. Which was odd, she thought, considering that he came from a very wealthy family back east and he was as traditional as they came in every other aspect. He'd made his own way up the corporate ladder with little or no help from his mother's family, was well-respected, and more than a little feared, which wasn't a bad thing in the business world. Be too nice and too respected and others tended to bulldoze over you.

He kept things on the up-and-up…for the most part.

Bryna chewed her bottom lip. She hadn't liked a couple of bits of info she'd picked up on him. And the fact that he was associated with Philippidis told her that he wasn't beyond selling himself to the highest bidder, no matter his own moral code.

Movement in the hall.

She quickly closed the laptop, only to watch as Elena waved at her as she passed, probably to visit Ari a few doors up.

She gave her a hello-how-do-you-do dismissive wave back.

Why did the woman set her teeth on edge whenever she saw her?

She sighed and opened her laptop again, reviewing what she'd written before saving it.

What she was avoiding very purposely when it came to Caleb was her own chaotic emotions related to what had passed between them the other night.

Quite simply, it was the best damn time she'd ever had.

With a man who was quite possibly even more commit-phobic than her cousin Troy.

She leaned back in her chair and closed her eyes. Since last Friday night, that's all it took for her to remember what it was like to lie in his bed, her back against his soft sheets, his hard body folded into hers.

He'd tried to call her yesterday. She knew that. Knew his number by heart. But she'd been at the brunch table with her cousins, uncle and Elena, nearly choking on her frittata when she'd glanced at her vibrating cell phone. In her hurry to clear the display in case Ari or Troy, who'd been sitting on either side of her, saw it, the expensive piece of equipment had sailed over the opposite side of the table and splintered into three pieces on the deck floor.

She still needed to run to the store to get a replacement.

More movement in the hall.

With a press of a button, she put the laptop to sleep and reached instead for the telephone, picking up the receiver to indicate she was busy.

Elena again.

She raised her hand to wave. But rather than merely returning it and continuing on, Elena stopped on the other side of the door and turned the knob.

Bryna grimaced as she pretended conversation with a supplier.

"That's unacceptable," she said to the dial tone. Afraid the other woman might hear it, she discreetly pushed a button that stopped the infernal sound. But she knew it was only a matter of time before a recording would play informing her to try her number again.

Elena stood smiling in front of her desk. "I'm sorry to interrupt..."

Bryna covered the mouthpiece. "I'm on the line with a supplier. I'm afraid I'm going to be a while."

"That's okay. I'll wait."

The other woman sat down in the single metal green plastic visitor's chair against the wall.

Great.

"What?" Bryna said into the phone. "That's not what I show." She sighed heavily. "Look, let me check my numbers and get back to you."

She hung up the phone just as it began that giveaway buzz indicating it was off the hook with no active call.

She smiled. "Hi, Elena. How are you?" She tried for casual.

"Fine. Listen, I don't want to bother you if you're busy, but Ari said something about you needing to run into town to replace the cell phone that broke yesterday, and suggested that since I'm going that way, I might want to offer you a ride. Perhaps we can catch some lunch, as well."

"Lunch?" Bryna said the word as if it were completely foreign to her.

She was about to offer up an excuse about having other plans, or an appointment, or something equally lame and transparent when Ari's handsome head popped into the doorway.

"There you are. I was afraid I missed you."

He came inside and Bryna watched Elena immediately get to her feet to face him. "Did I forget something?"

Ari's grin was so intimate that even Bryna felt compelled to look away. She quietly straightened already straight papers in her in-box.

"Just this," he said, and kissed Elena thoroughly.

Bryna sighed loudly unintentionally, noticing that the other woman was a little unsteady on her feet.

Ari chuckled. "Sorry for the PDA," he said to her. "So, are you girls going into town for lunch, then?"

Bryna opened her mouth to say no, but the look on his face and the hopeful expression that Elena wore stopped the word in its tracks.

"Give me five minutes?" she said to Elena.

"Sure. I'll meet you outside."

The sickeningly sweet couple left her office and Bryna flopped back in her old, squeaky chair, wondering how she got herself into these messes. And how she could go about getting herself out...

9

DRESSED IN SWEATPANTS and a Yale T-shirt, Caleb faked going right and went left, making his way easily around Palmer to earn a jump shot on the half court at his private downtown health club.

"So how's Cissy?" Palmer asked as he went out and caught the ball.

Caleb frowned. He'd forgotten he'd taken Cissy east with him a couple of months ago for some sort of charity event his mother had chaired. The visit had been so brief—overnight—that he'd barely registered it. "You'd probably be better off asking her."

"Ah." Palmer came at him straight on, hooking the ball and scoring before Caleb could get his hands up to block. "Have we reached the cutoff point already?"

Caleb grinned, taking the ball and making Palmer chase him. "How about you? Found yourself a lady to settle down with yet?"

"Settle down? What's that?"

Caleb had figured out fairly quickly a long time ago that one of the reasons the two of them got on so well was they were more similar than different. Ambitious to a fault. Career above all. They were brothers in arms in a world where everything else shifted and changed and often collapsed altogether.

"So it must be something important to bring you out here," Caleb said, claiming another point and then calling a time-out. He led the way to a nearby table and handed Palmer a bottle of iced water and opened one for himself. They toasted each other before taking a sip.

"Philippidis asked me to come out," his friend said.

Caleb's fingers tightened on the plastic bottle. "Since when have you been associated with Philippidis?"

"Since the economy suffered a massive sinkhole and all of us are forced to band together to insure our collective survival."

Caleb narrowed his eyes. Palmer's law firm was one of the most solvent out there. Not given to short-sighted investments or dealings. Surely he wasn't saying he was at risk?

"May I ask what kind of business you two are in together?" His throat tightened, nearly refusing the water he attempted to swallow. Why hadn't Philippidis told him there was a deal in the works with Palmer DeVoe?

Palmer ran his wrist across his forehead and then reached for a towel. "Nothing specific yet. I'm here to feel things out, as it were."

Caleb didn't buy it. Something more specific had to be behind his old friend's visit to bring him back to a place that he'd purposely avoided for fifteen years.

But if Palmer didn't want to tell him, there was nothing he could do to change his mind.

For now.

Caleb tossed him the ball and the two went at it again, with Palmer landing one before he could catch up. He took the ball back and went long, the sounds of their breathing echoing off the high ceiling.

"So are you interviewing for Cissy's position yet?" Palmer asked just as Caleb threw.

The ball hit the backboard and bounced off, no-where near the net.

"Oh! And he loses his composure," Palmer said, getting to the ball first and faking a left before going right around him. "So what's her name? Anyone I know?"

Despite the difference of two time zones, it wasn't an unusual question. In the circles in which they traveled, the pool of well-off singles was small and relatively shallow. Even if they didn't know a person directly, at some point they had likely come in con-tact with direct or extended family. In Cissy's case, her older sister had married a Harvard astrophysicist and now lived in the Boston suburbs with her family, so Palmer had actually met Cissy before he had, although the two had never dated.

In fact, Palmer dated so rarely—except for the requisite woman on his arm at certain events—Caleb had once inquired about his sexual preferences. Palmer had laughed so hard, he'd never had to ask again.

"No."

He left his friend to interpret his response any way he chose to.

No, he wasn't entertaining candidates to take the place Cissy had vacated.

No, he wasn't seeing anyone Palmer would know.

No, he had no interest in discussing the matter.

What had happened between him and the lovely Miss Metaxas was so far outside the norm of his experience that he was reluctant to lump her into some group, dismiss the night as just another one spent with a willing female.

At the same time, he wasn't ready to examine the time they'd spent together too closely. And he certainly wasn't anywhere near to sharing her name with anyone.

Palmer made another shot and then grabbed the ball again, holding it still at his side. "Ready to call it?"

Caleb blinked. He'd lost interest in the game the instant his thoughts had turned to Bryna, which was funny because he'd taken his friend up on the offer to play to get his mind off her.

But never let it be said that he'd pass on a challenge of this nature.

He took the ball. "Not on your life," he said, intent on making Palmer work for every shot....

BRYNA PARKED in an angled curb spot in the small, one-time quaint downtown of Earnest. Unable to come up with a reason not to go to lunch with Elena without being inexcusably rude, she'd found herself insisting that they take her car, because Elena's was an older model Caprice that looked two hundred miles away from a total breakdown.

"So many places are boarded up," Elena commented quietly next to her.

"Hmm?"

Bryna glanced at her pale face, then out at the line of one-time businesses that had thrived in the town only a few years ago. Now all that remained of the thirty or so storefronts was an old diner that had seen better times, two bars at opposing angles, a cell phone shop that took up only a quarter of the space of what had once been Hardy's Hardware, and Chelsea's coffee/book/art shop across the street.

It was a sad sight to see. Sadder still when she considered the families that had been hurt by the closings. Sure, they had all taken a hit when strip malls started popping up some twenty miles outside of town, with jumbo supermarkets stealing business from Pop's Market and DeVoe's General Store, and all but dealing a lethal blow to the town's pharmacist. But they'd muddled through the first year and had managed to come out on top, with residents growing weary of the long drive to the other stores, and Earnest businesses reeling them back in with town-wide discounts and savings programs devised by the mayor's office.

Then the mill was forced to close its doors four years ago, imported materials undercutting their ability to turn a profit and federal regulation twisting their arms behind their backs. Her uncle and Troy and Ari had run in the red for two years, trying desperately to find an alternative route, but finally had to admit defeat, giving employees six months' notice and another six months' severance before finally closing the mill's doors for good.

They'd all watched as the town's businesses followed suit, falling like dominos down the block, the closure of one contributing to the bankruptcy of the next.

Then it finally looked as if the deal that she and her cousins had worked so hard to put together with Philippidis was going to happen, like a flower emerging from a crack in the neglected sidewalk.

Until the woman next to her had slept with Ari the night before her wedding to Philippidis.

She took the key from the ignition. "I'm going to run into the communications store. I'll meet you at the diner."

Elena blinked at her. If Bryna had been a bit brusque, she figured she had cause to be. So many lives impacted by out-of-control hormones. It should be illegal.

She got out of the car and walked toward the store, not even glancing in Elena's direction as they parted ways. Too bad she hadn't insisted on driving separately. She could have feigned a forgotten business meeting, or urgent phone call, and gotten out of the lunch altogether. But not even she would consider leaving the pregnant woman to fend for herself.

Within twenty minutes she had a replacement phone, had even managed to have them transfer her phone book, and began walking in the direction of the diner.

It was midday and the rain clouds had briefly parted, allowing the summer sun to shine through, glinting against the wet pavement. She'd spent her teenaged years here in Earnest. Used to enjoy éclairs at the Steinway's Bakery that had closed last year. Attend hayrides and bonfires at Johnson's Feed and Weed located a few blocks north. Her entire adolescence had been shaped by a place that no longer existed.

A dull ache took up residence in her chest even as she felt renewed determination to turn things around.

"Bryna?"

She blinked at a woman standing in front of the

diner wearing a waitress uniform. "Jessica?" she said incredulously.

Jessica Talbot was an old classmate of hers. They were the best of friends one summer, until Jessica had gotten pregnant and married her seventeen-year-old boyfriend. She'd worked at the mill office for a year before it finally closed down.

Now, apparently, she was working at the diner.

And looked at least ten years older than Bryna rather than the same age.

"How are you?" She gave the other woman a quick, awkward hug. "God, it's been ages."

"Yes, it has. I don't think I've seen you since Jason's baptism…what, seven years ago?"

"Surely it can't be that long ago?"

"Wait. You're right. I think I ran into you at the mill once or twice. But we never got a chance to talk."

Bryna felt instantly guilty. She'd been so consumed with her own life at the time, which had been filled with Washington University classes, that she'd barely noticed her old friend.

And had Jessica not said anything, she might have walked right past her now.

A truck pulled up grill first at the curb and an older man in overalls got out, straightening his ball cap. "Jessica," he said, nodding.

She greeted him back and then the instant he was inside, said, "I've really got to get moving. I told Verna I'd be back in fifteen minutes. She'll throw a fit if I leave her in the lurch for too long during the lunch rush."

Bryna smiled. "Actually, I'll probably still be here when you get back. I'm meeting somebody for lunch."

"Oh."

Jessica didn't have to say that catching up had to done now. Upon her return she would go back to work—no time for conversation.

Bryna opened her purse and took out a card. "Here. My cell phone number's on the back. Call me. We'll get together for lunch or something."

She winced at the words, feeling their difference in stations in an acute way she'd never experienced before. She'd always been treated the same as anyone else when they were kids.

Now she was an outsider.

"Sure," Jessica said, already beginning to walk away. "I'll call you."

Bryna stood for a long time on the sidewalk, watching as Jessica hurried up the street and then turned the corner. Was she still living with her mother in the old clapboard house a few blocks up? She hadn't had a chance to ask. She hadn't seen a ring on her finger, but she didn't know if that meant that she'd taken it off for work, or if the marriage that had stood little chance of working had finally reached its end.

Someone waving from the diner window caught her eye. She frowned.

Elena.

God help her get through this lunch without blasting her soon-to-be cousin-in-law for every sin since the beginning of time. For ruining the deal with Philippidis. For making Troy work nonstop to save Metaxas Ltd. For ensuring the town of Earnest had to struggle for another year. But mostly for adding ten years to the young face of her one-time friend....

_10_

"YOU DIDN'T CALL ME BACK," Caleb's whiskey voice said when Bryna answered her cell.

She relaxed against the dozens of pillows that adorned her childhood bed at the Metaxas estate. For the first time in what felt like days, she smiled an indulgent smile, the sound of Caleb's naughty chuckle tickling more than her ear.

"You didn't leave a message requesting I call you back," she countered.

She debated telling him she'd had to replace her cell phone, then decided against it. Let him think what he wanted. All that mattered was that he had called again. Which meant that last Friday was more than a one-night affair to him.

She looked at her watch. It was a few minutes after ten and she'd just gone up to her room to get out of her work clothes and take a long bath with a good book when her new cell phone rang. It had taken four tries for her to find the right button to answer, bewildered by the latest in technology. Immensely frustrating, since she'd seen his name pop up in the extra-large display.

"Hard day?" he asked.

Bryna bit her bottom lip even as she slid her pumps off. "You have no idea. How about you?"

"No more difficult than any other Monday."

"So it was good, then."

"I never consider a day good. Only challenging or unchallenging. Successful or unsuccessful."

"Shocker."

As for her, her day had taken a nosedive when she'd run into Jessica and hadn't improved a bit from there.

She'd gone in to share a table with Elena only to quickly figure out that lunch had never been the intent all along. Rather, Elena had gone to the diner to confirm rumors that Verna, the owner, was looking to sell or close up shop. And to establish that Elena was interested in buying it.

Bryna couldn't have been more surprised. Yes, she'd known that Elena's family had been in the restaurant business. But Bryna hadn't even imagined that she might return to work. After all, she had seduced one of the state's most eligible bachelors in her cousin Ari. Why would she be interested in working? Especially considering she was preggers?

And Verna's restaurant, The Quality Diner, had been owned by her family for generations. Her grandfather had turned it into the mainstay it was now, making it crisis-proof. It was an Earnest landmark. Surely Elena didn't think it would be that easy to slip in with the locals?

Besides, Verna couldn't be seriously considering selling. The tall redhead might be getting up there in age, but she had two sons and a daughter that were a decade or two older than Bryna. Surely one of them would be interested in running the place? View the restaurant as their rightful legacy.

She began unbuttoning her blouse.

"What are you doing right now?" Caleb asked. "Right this moment?"

Bryna let the light material whisper down her arms. "Why? This couldn't actually be a booty call, now, could it?"

Caleb's burst of laughter told of his surprise. "That depends."

"On what?"

"On how quickly you can get over here."

She shivered from head to foot. "How about you come to me." She popped the catch on her skirt and kicked her legs until it lay on the floor along with her blouse. "I'm at home in Earnest."

"At the Metaxas Estate?"

"That would be home."

A long pause and then, "Oh."

She settled more comfortably against the pillows, one of which was covered with a needlepoint design of daisies that her mother had made just before the crash. "Do I detect a measure of disappointment, Mr. Payne?"

"You definitely detect a measure of disappointment."

She grinned against the mouthpiece. "Good."

"Sadist."

She could get used to this. To Caleb wanting her and not liking not being able to have her. She got the distinct impression that what Caleb Payne wanted he got. Period. No questions asked.

She could certainly attest to that. He was a difficult man to refuse.

Of course, she currently had no reason to turn away his flattering and exciting attentions.

She pursed her lips. "What makes you think I'd respond to your booty call anyway?"

"I never conceded that's what this is."

"Mmm. I'd say it is. What time is it? After ten. You're bored and you picked up the phone to find some company. I'd say that has booty call written all over it."

"All right, then. I concede."

She took a deep breath and released it slowly, wishing she could have responded to his call, gone to his place dressed in nothing but a raincoat and re-enacted the other night with a few new ideas thrown in for good measure. But she was in Earnest until Wednesday night. And unless he had reason to visit the small town—which wasn't a good idea any way you looked at it, because she'd never dare invite him to the house; her cousins would tar and feather him for sure—that meant that she wasn't going to see him until midweek at the earliest.

She told him when she'd be returning to the city and he responded with "Then I'll meet you at my place. Say at around seven?"

Bryna smiled. "Do you really think I'm that easy?"

"No. I'm saying I really want to see you that badly."

"Seven at your place, then. Wednesday."

The word caught in her mind, a niggling voice trying to tell her something. Then it occurred to her why. "Damn. I forgot. I already have a date for that night."

Silence.

She rubbed the arch of one foot against the front of the other, enjoying his speechless reaction.

"I could meet you after," she suggested playfully.

"You could meet me after your date?"

"Mmm-hmm."

He didn't sound pleased. Not pleased at all.

She laughed quietly. "I'm attending a charity ball that night. Something planned way in advance."

"And your date?"

She was surprised he'd asked outright. "My cousins."

She actually heard his sigh of relief.

Which was interesting. She didn't figure Caleb for

the possessive type. Especially considering that they weren't actually dating, much less anywhere near the stage of exclusivity. They'd slept together. Once.

Yet she couldn't help getting a little thrill at the thought that Caleb wanted her for himself.

"What celebrity event might that be?" he asked.

She told him.

"Funny, but I'm also scheduled to be in attendance."

"Is that right?"

"Yes."

"But you were willing to break the date in order to meet me at your place."

"Whereas you are unwilling."

"Only because my cousins view it as an extension of my job. You know, considering the urgency of our plans."

"Mmm."

"So I guess I'll see you there, then," she murmured.

"I guess you will."

"Will you be offering me a ride home afterward, do you think?"

"No."

She lifted her brows.

"I'll be offering you a ride to my place."

"Done."

"Good."

Why did she get the impression that everything

with Caleb was going to amount to a bartering session of sorts?

He cleared his throat. "You never did answer my question earlier…" he said leadingly.

"And which question might that be?"

"What you're wearing…"

"Mmm…you're right," she teased, slipping her free thumb under one bra strap. "How badly do you want to know?"

"Considering I can't see you until Wednesday? Very badly."

"And knowing I'm lying across my canopy bed wearing nothing but a lacy red bra and red panties is going to help?"

She heard his groan and shivered in response to his guttural reaction.

"Immensely."

She enjoyed the sexually charged silence for a few moments, then said, "Well, then, I suppose you might want to know what my right hand is doing right now, wouldn't you?"

"You have no idea…"

11

CALEB SAT ON THE PIANO BENCH before his Steinway grand, running his fingertips over the keys without making a sound as he listened to Bryna's tinkling laughter. He caught a reflection of himself in the glass picture windows, illuminated by the penthouse's soft recessed lighting. The city of Seattle was a constellation of twinkling lights against the dark. He'd taken off his suit coat and tie, rolled up the sleeves and unbuttoned the collar of his crisp broadcloth shirt. His shoulders were hunched slightly over the piano keys and he was…grinning.

The vision was so unusual as to be surprising. About this time of night he might be in his home office going over numbers or catching up on correspondence he'd missed over the course of the day if nothing else was on tap. Or even reading a business journal while watching news and enjoying a finger of whiskey.

Anything but what he was doing. Which was thoroughly enjoying a late-night conversation with Bryna Metaxas while a jazz CD played throughout the penthouse.

"Are you still there?" Her soft voice drifted into his eardrum like the note on the piano.

"I'm still here." He shifted on the bench.

"So do you want to know where my hand is?"

He envisioned her lying back on a big, rough-hewn canopy bed, her red undergarments contrasting against a thick white comforter, her skin smooth, her body curvy.

"Tell me," he said, his voice husky. He told himself it was from the whiskey, but not even he bought it.

"It's lying against my stomach, just above my navel…"

A sexy spot that he'd taken great pleasure in probing with the tip of his tongue last Friday.

"Oh, wait," she whispered. "It just moved…"

As did Caleb. He rose to his feet and neared the windows, trying to concentrate on the skyline.

"My fingertips are inching their way ever so slowly upward.…"

"I'd have opted for downward."

A soft laugh. "I wouldn't have thought you an impatient man, Caleb."

Normally, he wasn't. "I don't believe in wasting time."

She hummed. "And is that what you think we're doing? Wasting time?"

"Where is your hand now?"

Silence and then he heard a muffled sound as if she'd moved the phone. Or was, perhaps, stretching out more comfortably on the bed. "My palm just grazed my nipple through the lacy red fabric of my bra...."

His mouthed watered with the desire to claim that same sexy bit between his lips.

"My index finger is working its way under the bottom of the cup...." She hummed. "Naked flesh against naked flesh..."

His temperature rose a couple of degrees. "You read those steamy novels, don't you?"

"I had a date with one tonight, actually. In the bathtub."

She didn't play fair. He had an image of her covered up to her neck in silky bubbles, her skin rosy from the hot water, her nipples poking through, her red-painted toes gripping the opposite edge as her hands did Lord only knew what under the surface.

"Would you like me to continue? Or would you like me to recommend one of those novels?"

His throat was tight. "Continue. Please..."

"Mmm. That's what I thought you'd say...."

He turned from the windows and made his way to the sitting area of the living room, choosing one of the modern brown armchairs to sink down into. He was still facing the windows, as much of the furniture in the apartment was, designed to showcase the penthouse's view to its best advantage. He reached for a remote on the table in front of him and dimmed the overhead lighting until he was little more than a dark silhouette.

"Oops. Seems my hand has, um, a mind of its own. It's no longer satisfied with the juvenile fondling. It's undoing the catch on my bra and…" She sighed. "There. It's gone. Nothing to get in the way of a good, thorough caress…"

Caleb's erection twitched under the fabric of his pants.

"Where are you now?" she asked.

"In my apartment."

He heard her smile. "I know that. Where in your apartment?"

"In the living room."

"Facing the windows?"

"Uh-huh. Sitting in a chair. I was at the piano, but I relocated while you were talking."

"Feeling a bit restless, Mr. Payne?"

A bit didn't come near to covering it.

"And are you…turned on by my verbal exploration?"

"I would be if you shut up and got on with it."

Her laughter touched something deep inside him. "My. We are the impatient one tonight, aren't we?"

If *impatient* meant he was ready to grab his car keys and make his way to Earnest in record time, then, yes, he was very impatient.

"My question to you," she murmured. "Where is *your* free hand?"

"Gripping the arm of the chair. Tightly."

"Mmm…let's see if we can't change that.…"

He settled more comfortably into the chair, *comfortable* being a relative term.

"I'm propping the phone against the pillows because one hand just isn't doing it for me…" she said.

Caleb swallowed hard, seeing her run her palms over her full, pert breasts.

"My nipples are so, so hard.… I'm licking my fingers.… Mmm, yes. I can almost imagine that it's your tongue flicking across them.…"

Her voice had dropped to a whiskey whisper, encouraging him to follow her into the fantasy she was creating with her words.

He reached down to rearrange his throbbing hard-on in his pants.

"Bad right hand…bad," she said.

Caleb's swallow sounded louder than it should have. "What's bad right hand doing?" he couldn't help asking when she didn't immediately continue.

"Bad right hand is leaving my breasts and sliding slowly, ever so slowly, down my trembling stomach…"

The penthouse around Caleb disappeared, leaving him in an isolated cocoon.

"Oh…oh…" she whispered.

"Tell me," he insisted roughly.

"Bad li'l right hand is cupping me through my panties." He heard her licking her lips and found himself doing the same thing. "My legs are spreading open…yes…"

Before he realized his hand had moved, it had undone the catch on his slacks and tugged down the zipper, not stopping until he clutched his own flesh in his palm.

"The crotch of my panties is dripping with desire…"

Christ, she was going to be the end of him.

He tried to think of the last time he'd even thought about jacking off. Surely not since he was a teenager, before he'd discovered that with a little effort he could have a willing female look after the task for him. But his brain was shutting down, denying him the luxury of rational thought as he slid easily into the sensual web of sensation Bryna created for him.

Her voice sounded raspier still. "My index finger just tunneled under the elastic…mmm…yes. It's stroking the length of my swollen, hungry lips…"

"What's she hungry for?" he asked.

"Why you, Mr. Payne."

Caleb sank down farther into the chair, his arousal standing upright, almost angrily, from the V of his open slacks. He gripped the hard flesh, taken aback by the instant, jerking response.

"I…have…to…take…these…off.…"

She was stripping off her panties. Dear Lord.

"Oh, yessss…"

His mouth went suddenly dry. "Describe the sensations for me, Bry."

"It's… I…"

"Try…"

"The cool air hitting my dampness is so, so sweet.…"

He could see her lying spread-eagled, her knees bent, her womanhood bared to him.

"I'm shaking all over…" she whispered.

Amazingly, so was he.

His grip tightened and he drew his hand upward than down again, his mind's eye filled with the image of her parted lips, her pupil-dominated eyes.

"I'm running my hands up the inside of my thighs…no…not yet." He detected the restless chaos in her voice. "I want this to last a little longer…"

Caleb brought his foreskin up over his aching head of his penis and brought it back down, his own gut tightening.

"So wet…so very slick…"

She was stroking herself.

"Oh…oh…oh!"

"Pinch your clit for me, Bry."

"I…can't…"

His own crisis was nearing the boiling point.

"I…it's so sensitive…so hard…"

Caleb's hips bucked involuntarily.

"Oh, yessssss," she hissed.

Her soft cries filled his ear as he came right along with her.

BRYNA LAY SPENT and gasping for breath against the pillows. She'd lost the cell phone at some point but didn't have the energy to search for it just then. She slowly lifted her hand and ran it over her face and hair, unable to believe she'd done what she had. She'd never been so blatantly uninhibited before. But something about Caleb coaxed something out from within her. Something more elemental…more sexual…more animalistic.

She heard a muffled sound and realized it was probably him on the phone.

She rolled over to fish it out from where it had dropped between two pillows.

"Bryna? Are you still there?"

Her smile was so large it nearly hurt her face muscles. "I'm still here. You?"

His sexy chuckle washed over her like a touch.

She lifted herself on her elbows and swayed her feet in the air, pressing her hips tightly against the mattress. Another shiver wend through her.

"So, tell me, Mr. Payne. Did I bring you any pleasure tonight?"

"You brought me a great deal of pleasure."

"But?"

"But it's nowhere near the kind of pleasure I'd like to show you Wednesday night."

She was filled with hot anticipation. "Promises, promises."

"Oh, no, Bry. I don't make promises. I make plans."

"Well, then. I have to say I'm more than a little intrigued."

"How much more?"

"A lot."

A comfortable silence stretched between them as she laid her head down, cradling the phone between her ear and a pillow.

"Would you like to have another go at it?" she whispered. "This time with you in charge of the verbal tour?"

"I'm afraid I wouldn't be nearly as effective as you."

She smiled and found herself yawning. "I find that hard to believe."

He chuckled. "I think this is the part where I bid you a fond good-night, Miss Metaxas."

"Mmm. Good night."

"Sweet dreams."

"Sleep tight."

She reluctantly disconnected the call and tossed the cell to the opposite side of the bed. If he made an appearance in her dreams, they would be very sweet indeed....

12

WEDNESDAY MORNING finally dawned sunny and warm, but Bryna suspected that the day would drag by like an eternity if it was anything like yesterday.

She'd never really gotten into poetry, but a half-remembered fragment from the passage of time rang so true that she'd begun pulling various volumes out of the Metaxas library in search of it. Strangely, rather than help her get through the day, the quest seemed to make the time go even slower.

Of course, the fires that had sparked at work yesterday hadn't helped. The company's head engineer and his five-man team, who were working on retainer until Metaxas Limited secured the funds to continue with their plans, had come in and asked to be released from their contract. It seemed another, rival company was offering him double what they were paying.

It didn't take more than a few phone calls to

confirm their suspicions that Manolis Philippidis was behind the move.

Without the head engineer, they could still squeak by, but not without his team. If all of them left, there would be no moving forward anywhere, with or without funds.

Bryna had stayed late, along with Troy and Ari and a handful of other longtime Metaxas employees, discussing their strategy. If they tried to force the men to honor the contract, they might sue to get out, creating lots of bad blood on both sides. They considered meeting the amount Philippidis offered, no matter how difficult it would be for them to do. And finally placed on the table was the alternative of just letting them go.

Silence had been the response from all.

Now she was snatching a moment of peace with a bowl of Cocoa Puffs and a book of Thoreau's, after spending much of last night working out how she was going to move forward with her own clandestine plans with Caleb, both on a professional and a personal level.

Ari settled himself next to her at the kitchen counter, sighing. Which was never a good thing, because Ari never sighed. Even at the daylong meetings yesterday, he'd never given up hope that they would reach some sort of compromise with the engineers. He'd talk to them, he said, get them to realize that taking Philippidis's offer might appeal in the short term, but in the long, they'd be setting themselves up for disappointment and frustration.

Bryna lifted the spoon to her mouth as Ari sighed for a third time, turning her cereal to little more than chocolate chalk. She finally put her book down and stared sidelong at him as she chewed. After swallowing, she said, "I'm sure I'm going to live to regret this, but what is it?"

His answering grin made her want to swat him with her book. "Elena thinks she's done something to insult you."

"She did. She met you."

Troy entered the kitchen and poured himself a glass of orange juice, and then one for Ari when he asked for it. "She's got you there, Ari."

Bryna smiled triumphantly.

While the three of them getting up together and sharing breakfast had been a regular occurrence a few months ago, lately they seemed to leave the house in stages. Troy was getting up at Lord knew what hour (Bryna suspected that he'd actually slept at the office more than a few nights), while Ari got in late after spending what time he could with Elena every evening. Which left her on her own to eat in a quiet kitchen, as her uncle's summer schedule wrapped around tee-off times that saw him coming and going.

"What are you still doing staying here, anyway?" Bryna asked Ari. "Shouldn't you two lovebirds be shacked up together somewhere? Especially considering that you've already knocked her up?"

Troy broke a couple of eggs into a hot pan. "Can you bring the language up just this side of the gutter?"

She gave him an eye roll. "Don't shoot the messenger. Acknowledge the message."

Troy looked at Ari. "She has a point."

Ari pointed toward the pan. "Smells good. Make a couple for me?"

"If you put on the toast."

"Deal." Ari got up and took a loaf of wheat bread from a drawer, feeding four slices into the eight-piece toaster. "You want one?" he asked her.

"Pass. Thanks."

"Don't mention it. Anyway, the reason why Elena and I aren't living together yet is that she wants to wait until we're married."

"And then?" Troy asked.

Ari stared at him. "Then, what?"

"Oh, God," Bryna said, losing her appetite altogether. Which was tough considering this had always been her favorite cereal. "You're not going to move her in here, are you?"

Ari aimed a glare in her direction. Another rare occurrence that left Bryna feeling guilty. "As luck would have it, Elena doesn't think it's a good idea. But I haven't given up trying. This place is big enough for five full-size families."

Bryna sighed with relief. "I don't think I've given her enough credit."

"Which is exactly the point I'm trying to make," Ari said, pointing at her. "She said you were awfully quiet during lunch the other day."

Bryna got up and dumped the remnants of her bowl down the sink drain and ran the water. "Quiet is better than saying what was on my mind. Trust me."

Troy turned his eggs onto a plate and broke another couple into the pan. "What happened?"

"Happened? Oh, nothing. It was a perfectly nice lunch at The Quality Diner. I caught up with a couple of friends. Was reminded how Verna's open-face roast beef sandwich used to rank as my favorite food group. And then it dawned on me that lunch wasn't the only thing on Elena's agenda."

"How do you mean?"

She sighed. "She wants to buy the place."

The toast popped up, startling Ari. "She doesn't want to buy the place. She was just curious to see if the rumors were true."

"The Quality?" Troy said. "But the Burns have owned that place forever."

Ari took butter out of the refrigerator. "And Verna apparently is feeling as old as the restaurant. Word has it that if the right offer comes along she'll take it."

Troy raised his brows. "What about her kids?"

"Exactly what I want to know," Bryna agreed,

crossing her arms as she stood next to Troy, facing off with Ari from across the island.

He eyed the pan. "You're going to burn those." Troy turned the eggs out onto a fresh plate. "You two are making it sound like this is some kind of conspiracy. Elena isn't doing anything illegal. We're going to be married. She's going to be moving here to Earnest. The only restaurant within a thirty-mile radius is The Quality. And if Verna wants to sell... well, it's as simple as that."

Bryna and Troy stared at him.

"Is she going to buy it?" Bryna asked.

"I'd prefer she didn't," Ari said under his breath, buttering and cutting the toast and then putting the plates in front of two stools on the counter. "Look, I may not like the idea—for entirely different reasons than you—but if it's one thing I've learned, it's that Elena doesn't live by anybody's rules but her own."

"Shocker," Bryna said.

Ari took his seat and accepted the eggs Troy slid his way. "Thanks. And thanks a lot." He sighed heavily. "Elena said this was going to take some time, but, Christ, will you hurry up and get over yourself? We're getting married and there's going to be another Metaxas in seven months."

Troy took his stool next to his brother as Bryna replied, "Maybe if you stopped trying to shove her down our throats, I'd stop reacting as if that's what you were doing."

Ari glowered. "No, Bryna. Shoving her down your

throats would be moving her in here and having her fix breakfast for us all every morning. And dinner every night. And including her in every activity."

Bryna shot Troy a horrified look.

"And if you guys don't start showing some more respect for my wife-to-be, then I swear I'll start doing just that."

Bryna raised her hands in surrender. "I think that's my cue to leave."

Troy took a sip of juice. "Since we're all up, I thought we might drive in together."

Bryna squinted at him. "Sorry. I'll pass."

She rounded the island and kissed each of them on the cheek, her last cousinlike move of the day; from here on out everything would switch to business. "I'm going to have to leave work early in order to get to Seattle in time to make my hair appointment."

Ari blinked at her. "Hair appoint… Damn. I forgot all about that damn charity event tonight."

Bryna tried not to beam. She hadn't forgotten. It was all she'd been able to think about.

"Don't even consider ducking out of it," Troy said. "I need all three of us there. I'll give you a list of the people we need to split up and talk to."

"We already have it," Bryna said.

"I've updated it."

This time she and Ari shared a long-suffering look. "Why am I not surprised?"

"What do you mean—"

"See you at the office, guys. Enjoy your breakfast."

She walked out of the kitchen as quickly as she could without seeming in too much of a hurry, thinking that all would be perfect if she could just fast-forward through the day and have it be night....

IT WAS DIFFICULT TO STAND in the living area of his penthouse without recalling the other night and his risqué phone conversation with Bryna. From the piano bench to the windows to the chair, each made him remember her whispered words and the sizzling impact they'd had on him.

The woman was definitely an intriguing puzzle to be pieced together. She took up more of his thoughts than any of the women he'd dated before combined.

Caleb straightened his tux jacket and checked his cufflinks, turning the idea over in his mind. A warning voice sounded in the back of his head. A voice he ignored. At least for now.

He glanced at his watch, surprised to see he was early. The event didn't start for another half hour. And he made it a point to always arrive late at such gatherings.

He smiled and walked to the bar. He opened a bottle of sparkling water, poured a bit into an etched crystal glass and took a sip. His lack of access to the maddening woman could be partially to blame for his obsession with her. To have had a taste and then be denied seconds was a situation he wasn't used to. He generally opted for uncomplicated women who would rearrange their plans in order to put him first.

But Bryna…

Complicated. Very definitely complicated.

And very definitely irresistible.

The sound of the doorbell filled the room. He looked in the direction of the entry area. Bryna, unable to wait?

The possibility presented all sorts of options on how they might fill the time between now and the charity ball.

He began walking toward the door, but Lionel beat him to it.

"I'll see to it, sir."

Caleb stretched his neck and checked his cufflinks again. "Of course."

He walked back toward the window, glass in hand, attempting nonchalance when all he wanted was to turn and watch her enter the room.

Unfortunately, it wasn't Bryna there to surprise him. It was his mother.

"Is that expression any way to welcome your mother, Caleb?" Phoebe Payne asked with a perfumed smile. "Get over here and give me a hug already, will you? Before I develop a complex…"

13

"IF I DIDN'T KNOW BETTER, I'd think my little surprise visit is unwelcome," Phoebe said as they rode in the limo to the Seattle Center.

Caleb stared out the window at the raindrops that dotted the glass and turned the streets and sidewalks into a dark, shiny mirror that reflected buildings and cars. "Don't be ridiculous, Mother. You are always welcome."

She finished freshening up her lipstick and slid him an amused look. "Now, that was convincing."

Caleb tucked his chin into his chest and chuckled. "I'm sorry. I don't mean to offend you. You know how I feel about surprises."

She tucked her compact back into her clutch and sat back, sliding her hand onto his arm. "I know. That's why I make it a point to keep springing them on you."

Complicated.

Caleb recalled using the same word to describe Bryna even as he looked into the aging but still beautiful face that belonged to his mother. She'd gone completely blonde about eight years ago when, she claimed, she'd surrendered in her battle against gray. It had taken her a few wrong shades to hit the right one, but somehow the golden hue of her almost girlish curls suited her. It helped that she took good care of herself, exercising regularly, watching her weight and getting a discreet nip, tuck, or collagen shot every now and again.

It still boggled the mind that she had never married. Oh, she'd come close a time or two. Even been engaged once when he was thirteen. But when Caleb had voiced his disapproval of the groom-to-be, she'd dropped the man like a hot potato, automatically choosing her son and only child over marriage to a man he didn't like, no matter the reason.

The experience had taught him an important lesson about male-female relationships. Mainly that he could manipulate them, bend them to his will.

And he'd been doing it ever since.

"So will your date be meeting us there?" his mother inquired.

He looked at her. She never referred to the women he dated by name. He'd asked her once why and she'd simply shrugged and said there was no use becoming friendly with someone who would soon be replaced by another.

"And what happens if I ever meet someone who's more than a date?"

She'd raised a perfect eyebrow, considering him for a long moment. "Well, then I guess I'll have to learn her name."

"How will you know?"

She'd laughed quietly. "Oh, I'll know."

"I see. Because you're an expert in matters of the heart."

She'd flinched and he regretted what was meant as a gentle barb. "No. Because I'm an expert on my son."

His formative years hadn't been bad ones. His mother's family had been wealthy, so he'd never lacked for anything and had been brought up in the same house in which she'd been raised, surrounded by extended family. And Phoebe, herself, had been an understanding mother, almost eerily intuitive if not especially doting. She'd always been there when he'd needed her. And did seem to know him better than anyone else, no matter how he often tried to convince himself differently.

"So what brings you out this way?" he asked.

"What? It's not enough that I want to see my one and only child every now and again?"

He smiled. "I'm too much like you to buy that."

"Yes, I guess you are. And I'm still trying to determine if that's a good or bad thing."

"The charity event?"

"Oh, heavens, no. We have plenty of these back east."

"So?" he asked when she didn't continue.

This time she looked out the window. "I've met someone."

Caleb raised his brow at her.

What were the chances that they both would meet someone special within the same time span after having spent so many years happily single?

"And this someone might be?"

She patted his arm and then withdrew her hand. "Now, if I told you, I'd likely jinx the entire thing."

He couldn't help his chuckle. "I've never known you to be the superstitious type, Mother."

The smile on her soft mouth loomed in her eyes. "Lately I find myself wondering if I even know myself as well as I thought."

"As a result of this gentleman?"

She checked her hair. "Who said it was a man?"

Caleb coughed.

His mother laughed. "I always said you were a bit on the stodgy side. Never knew where you picked it up."

Seeing as he'd been raised in one of the most conservative families in the east, despite his mother's rather rebellious behavior when she'd borne him out of wedlock and never married, he guessed he could have learned the behavior from any one of a hundred people that had surrounded him. His maternal grandfather, the late, great industrialist Bedford Payne high up on that list.

"Certainly not from you," he agreed.

"Certainly not."

It wouldn't surprise him if his mother had taken a lady lover. But he got the impression she was pulling his leg, as she had a habit of doing just to get a rise out of him.

Still, he found it curious that she wasn't willing to share her love interest's name.

More curious still that he wasn't willing to share Bryna's name with her...

THE MAN WAS HOTTER than any one man had a right to be.

Bryna stood across the room from the door of the large hall, yet knew the instant Caleb entered. She felt the sensitive skin at the nape of her neck tingle as every nerve ending went on alert. She somehow managed to continue her conversation with one of the matriarchs of Seattle society and the chairwoman of the night's events, but Lord only knew how. Caleb filled her every sense, every thought.

He wore a tux that fit him like a second skin, emphasizing the width of his shoulders, the narrowness of his hips. His smile was wide and generous, his eyes dark and dangerous.

She shivered just knowing that tonight she would again be the recipient of his demanding kiss.

On his arm was a woman who didn't look that much older until they moved a little closer.

"Ms. Payne and Mr. Payne," Ari said at her elbow.

"What?"

"The woman and man that just came in."

"They're married?" she asked, already knowing the answer. Still, it wouldn't hurt to throw her cousin off the scent she was sure she radiated like a perfume.

She wanted Caleb. And she wanted him now.

Ari chuckled. "No. Mother and son. Only son. And some story there, from what I understand."

"Oh?"

A part of Bryna was turned off by inviting gossip related to a man she was seeing, however clandestinely. Another wanted to know every bit of information she could lap up about him.

"Well, Caleb isn't known as The Bastard Payne for no reason," her cousin said.

Troy neared them, deep in conversation with a patron of the arts, and if he had anything to say about it, a patron of Metaxas Limited's future plans.

But not deep enough that he couldn't spare a "Circulate. Circulate," as he walked by.

"Did you hear that?" Ari asked.

"What? The crack of the whip?"

He chuckled. "That would be it." He plucked a champagne flute from the tray of a passing waiter. "Enough fun. Time to do some business."

The problem was, the moment Caleb entered, everything but business was on Bryna's mind. Unless it was monkey business. But there was nothing juvenile about her attraction to Caleb. To the contrary, her thoughts were very, very adult.

"Good evening…Miss Metaxas, isn't it?" Caleb said, standing before her before she'd realized he'd moved across the room.

"Mr. Payne. Nice to see you again." She looked to the woman still on his arm. "Hello. I'm Bryna Metaxas."

The way she lifted her brows was awfully familiar. Bryna realized it was because Caleb did the exact same thing.

"Phoebe Payne. Caleb's mother." She offered her gloved hand and Bryna lightly squeezed her fingers, as was expected at these events. America might not have royalty, much to the chagrin of many in this very room, but they did have a number of wealthy, longstanding families that expected to be treated as such. "A pleasure to meet you."

"Metaxas…that's Greek, isn't it?"

"Yes. I'm third generation Greek-American."

Phoebe sighed. "I adore Greece. I try to get to the islands at least once every couple of years."

Caleb's dark eyes trapped Bryna's. She ordered herself to look everywhere but at him, but found she couldn't escape. Nor did she want to. Reflected in the depths she saw decadent scenes from the last time they were together. Heard her own sighs. Felt his hands on her hips, holding her still as he drove deep into her.

Phoebe Payne cleared her throat. "Caleb, darling, haven't I taught you it's impolite to stare?"

Bryna dropped her gaze, feeling as guilty as if the words had been said to her.

"You're quite right, Mother," he agreed. "But no one ever accused me of being polite."

Phoebe's laugh was low and musical.

"If you'll excuse me," Bryna said, "I've just been ordered to circulate by my overbearing cousin." She nodded her head. "Pleasure to make your acquaintance, Ms. Payne."

Phoebe looked between her and her son, her smile as knowing as any Caleb had ever given her. "I believe the pleasure is all mine, Miss Metaxas."

Rather than homing in on the next target on the list Troy had given her, Bryna headed for the back of the room and the buffet table instead. Why did she suddenly feel as if she'd been put through a head-to-foot MRI? Her pulse was racing, her palms were damp. It seemed she'd completely underestimated her ability to remain detached in public when it came to the sinfully handsome Caleb Payne.

As EXPECTED, Caleb's mother didn't stick with him for long. She had too many friends' cheeks to kiss, too much gossip to share and to hear. They parted ways shortly after he introduced her to Bryna. Which was a good thing, because he was finding it impossible to concentrate on anything other than the snug fit of her scarlet-red dress. It was made of an unforgiving material that would show every flaw unless you had the type of tight body to show off. And Bryna definitely had that body. An hourglass shape that found him taking in the roundness of her breasts, then the fullness of her hips, and back again.

A hand landed on his shoulder. "Looking for a Cissy replacement?" Palmer asked, stepping up next to him and following his gaze.

Caleb frowned and sipped at his champagne even as he looked for a waiter who might bring him something more his style. "Actually, I think I'm going to fly solo for a while." He offered up a grin. "Serial monogamy is taking its toll on me, I think."

"I wouldn't know."

"Of course you wouldn't. You never date the same woman twice."

Palmer looked down at his feet, smiling. "Yes. Something like that."

Caleb began walking and Palmer followed suit.

"You didn't say anything about coming here tonight," Caleb commented.

They'd met at the basketball court over lunch for a sweat-producing one-on-one. "Neither did you."

He chuckled. "No, I guess I didn't. I suppose I've been a little preoccupied lately."

His gaze lingered on Bryna, who was speaking to a matronly woman dripping in pearls. She had her back slightly turned, offering up a tantalizing view of her high, pert bottom, and a smooth length of leg through a side slit.

"And I think I may have just uncovered the cause," Palmer murmured.

Caleb looked at him sharply. "What's that?"

Palmer's eyes opened slightly at the unexpected reaction. "Hey, not my business."

"You're damn right it's not your business."

Palmer shifted him so they were walking in the other direction, his arm across his shoulders so he could speak quietly into his ear.

"I'm just going to say this only once, Caleb. I think it important that you heed it."

His shoulders tightened under Palmer's arm.

"Getting involved with a Metaxas when you have so much riding on Philippidis is not a good idea."

Caleb tried for an amused chuckle. Or at the very least, a smile. Instead, he found himself scowling darkly at his old friend. "My, but you've caught up to speed in a short amount of time."

Palmer stared at him evenly. "Think about how I did that, my friend."

Philippidis.

Caleb recalled Bryna's running into the old man last week.

"That's right. Philippidis suspects something's going on between the two of you. And while I wasn't asked outright to find out what it was, I was discreetly requested to unearth as much information as I could."

Bastard.

They neared the end of the group and stopped, turning to face each other.

"You're not a lover, Caleb. You're a warrior. Remember that. Many men have failed because of a woman. Don't be one of them."

"What the fuck do you know about it?" he asked.

Palmer's gaze dropped. "I know more than you know, buddy. I know more than you...."

14

IT WAS THREE IN THE MORNING, and Caleb had spent the better part of the evening making love to the slumbering woman sprawled naked across his bed in the other room.

Why, then, was he filled with so much restless energy? Why did he still want to go in there and wake her up and start all over again?

Wearing only a pair of drawstring pants, he sat at the piano, the overhead lights turned down to their dimmest setting, his fingers traveling over the keys, one time slowly, then transitioning into a difficult Liszt sonata, and yet again into Chopin. He didn't need sheet music. And didn't play a piece through till the end. He allowed the shadowy, chaotic emotions pulsing within to flow from his fingertips and into the piano.

It had been a good long while since he'd played for more than a few minutes to keep his fingers limber.

Now, eyes closed, his hair fell across his brow and he felt sweat begin to accumulate between his shoulder blades. Like the pieces that he played, snippets of conversations streamed through his mind, nonsensical, little more than gibberish when linked together, but all a part of a whole, a roadmap of sorts leading to a destination foreign to him.

He knew she was there before he saw her.

Caleb opened his eyes. He saw her shadowy reflection in the glass. Like the other night, she was wearing his white dress shirt, the hem hanging to just above her knees, her dark hair a cloud around her sexy face.

He swallowed deeply and continued playing, transitioning into *Moonlight Sonata*.

He felt her hand on his shoulder and tensed, his playing becoming more frenetic.

What was it about this one woman that drove him to distraction? That made him forget about everything but his need to fold himself into her? To claim her mind, body and soul?

He couldn't remember a time when he'd been so moved by another person, much less a woman.

And an alarm of warning sounded deep within him that he didn't want to feel it now.

He abruptly stopped playing and grasped her wrist, pulling her until she lay across his lap, her elbow hitting the keys, filling the room with a discordant din. Surprise rounded her soft mouth, her eyes large in her face.

"I...I thought you never played for anyone?"

Caleb set his jaw, remaining silent as he scanned her face. There was nothing special there. Broken down, her features were fairly normal. But when she smiled, when she spoke, when she called out his name in the heat of climax, she was an object of unbearable beauty.

She lifted a hand to his hair, smoothing it back from his brow. "It's so...haunting."

Haunting.

The word was fitting. For it was as if she was haunting him. Had slid just so under his skin. Always there. Always tempting his senses. Challenging his control.

She leaned forward and kissed him, her lips impossibly sweet.

Caleb kissed her back. Allowing himself a moment without that control he always tried so hard to keep in check.

Before too long, they were both gasping for breath. Bryna repositioned herself so that she straddled him on the bench, the keys she bumped emitting muffled, serene sounds.

She laughed almost silently and then pressed her nose against his, her hands in his hair. "I'm afraid I'm falling in love with you, Mr. Payne," she murmured.

Caleb's heart contracted to the point of pain.

All this was happening too fast. Outside any sort

of timeline he could have envisioned. Beyond any capacity for him to imagine.

He grasped her hips and lifted her to lie on top of the closed piano. Her feet tickled the keys as he held her down with one hand on her stomach. He stood and pushed the hem of his shirt up, spreading her legs, baring her to his hungry gaze.

They'd spent the past four hours in his bed. Surely his appetite for her should have been long since sated.

Yet he wanted her as if for the first time, his balls heavy, his erection so hard it hurt.

Still holding her down, despite her wiggling attempts to free herself, he splayed the fingers of his free hand against the skin just above her womanhood. He swept the pad of his thumb back and forth and then tunneled into her curls, pressing hard against her swollen clit.

She gasped and bucked against his hold, her breathing ragged, her hands reaching for the one that held her still.

"Please," she whispered. "I want to touch you."

He ignored her plea, instead parting her engorged folds with his thumb and finger, taking in the pink portal. His mouth filled with the desire to taste her, to taste them. Instead, he thrust two fingers deep inside her and twisted them around.

She moaned and instantly tried to close her legs, holding him inside her. He released his hold on her stomach and forced her knees back open, thrusting his fingers deep inside her again as she struggled against her own emotions and his touch.

His hard-on throbbed and burned with the need to bury himself inside of her. But he had no condoms on him. They were back in the bedroom where he had left her.

But she had come into the living room, invaded his longing for privacy, for space to put a name to what he was feeling, to find a way to control it.

She tried to sit up and he held her back down. But looking at her in her confused, turned-on state threatened to rip him to shreds.

He could carry her back to the bedroom. But he didn't want to wait that long.

So he pulled her forward, stripped her of his shirt and turned her over so that her bottom was lifted high in the air.

The position allowed him a different perspective. Her tight bottom. Her soft, fleshy womanhood.

He grit his teeth and grabbed her hips, hauling her to the edge of the piano.

This time when his fingers breached her, it wasn't in the place she was expecting. She tightened up on him and cried out. Caleb held himself totally still, leaving his finger where it was until he felt her muscles relax. Slowly he withdrew, moistening the digit with her own juices before returning to forbidden territory.

This time when he entered her, she was ready, her moan low and deep. She remained still, as if not trusting herself to move. Caleb flicked his thumb over the tight nub of her clit and she shivered. He moved his finger slowly in and out, then replaced one finger with two.

Dark desire filled him. A fundamental need to claim her in a way that no man had before. To stamp her in a unique way that would remain with her forever.

He undid the tie on his pants, letting the silky material drop down around his ankles. His member stood in hard relief. He grasped the base of his penis and rubbed the tip of his member along her slick flesh, and then positioned the head against her virginal opening. He gently pushed forward.

Her gasp was part pleasure, part pain as her tight muscles both invited him in and rejected him.

Using every shred of self-control he still possessed, he remained still. So very still. Waiting for her to adjust. For her to open to him. Accept him. Welcome the joining he sought.

Holding her hips still with one hand, he reached round her with the other, slowly stroking her liquid heat. She relaxed almost immediately, opening the way for him to enter her further.

Finally he was in to the hilt.

Jesus...

"Ohhhhh." The sound coming from Bryna's throat was guttural, feral. It reached inside him, grabbing him hard, making his pulse pound, his lungs refuse air. He slowly withdrew and entered her again. She shivered all over, her right hand blindly grasping his hip, holding him in deep.

Her reaction, combined with his heightened sense of arousal, sent him careening over the edge of reason. But rather than hold still, allow the climax free rein, he withdrew again and entered, withdrew again and entered, drawing out his orgasm and causing hers....

LONG AFTER THEY'D RETIRED back to the bedroom, after Caleb had finally drifted off to sleep, Bryna lay curved against him, listening to the sound of his heartbeat. She'd never been made love to so thoroughly. Had never been taken to the heights he'd introduced her to tonight. She felt at one with everything around her...yet oddly apart.

She'd seen a different side of Caleb tonight. A dark, demanding one. She'd glimpsed in his eyes a fierce, deep need that had held her entranced and scared her away all at once.

She understood that he was ruthless in the business arena. But up till now he'd been wonderfully open with her sexually. Tonight she'd realized that the demons that compelled him to succeed at business haunted him on every level.

He'd demanded everything from her. And she'd given it to him.

She was unfamiliar with this Bryna. With the woman who even as she questioned his need to possess her, opened to him nonetheless. He hadn't responded when she'd been compelled to whisper her confession that she believed she might be falling in love with him.

She squeezed her eyes shut. Of course he hadn't. He wasn't a man given to verbal declarations of affection. In fact, she was pretty sure he'd never uttered the words to a woman who wasn't his mother in his life. Or, if he had, he'd been deeply burned as a result.

Too fast…too much…

She bit hard on her bottom lip.

Never had she been swept away so quickly by her emotions. Fallen so hard for a man in such a short time. But she hadn't considered putting on the brakes. It had all been so new. So much fun.

Until now.

Now…

Bryna's heart beat an irregular rhythm in her chest.

Now she was afraid that she wasn't just falling in love with Caleb. But that she already loved him.

And feared that as a result, he wasn't going to welcome her in, draw her closer. He was going to push her away.

The thought was enough to make her feel as if her heart had just cracked into two jagged pieces.

Caleb moved in his sleep. She reluctantly shifted to give him room as he turned away from her.

She lay for long moments, staring at the strong, masculine lines of his back. She longed to snuggle up to him. Hold him for as long as he would allow her.

Instead, she gathered whatever bits of pride she still had left and slipped from the bed.—realizing as she did so that he wasn't asleep at all. Instead, he watched silently as she gathered her clothes and shoes and left the room, deciding to dress in the main bathroom rather than the master. Because she didn't want to have to pass him again. Feel the chest-crushing sensation.

He had withdrawn from her to a place where she'd never be able to reach him again.

15

"Okay, I've been droning on for twenty minutes and you haven't heard a single word I've said."

Caleb had been looking at his mother, but now brought her into full focus, his thoughts turned more inside than out.

"I'm enjoying my meal," he said.

He'd reluctantly agreed to meet her for lunch, giving in when she'd played the mother guilt card. "I'm only in town for a couple of days. Lord only knows when we'll see each other again. Speaking of which, when are you going to come back home to the east coast, anyway?"

That question should have told him to do whatever he had to to get out of the lunch date, but she was right. He didn't see her nearly enough. And was it too much to ask to spend an hour of uninterrupted time in her company?

Of course, he'd had no idea when he'd agreed that

his mind would be on other things. More specifically on Bryna.

He rubbed his face with his hands and reached for his water glass.

"So...that Bryna seemed like a nice girl," his mother said.

He nearly choked on the water. He narrowed his gaze, taking in Phoebe's far too smug expression. "Interesting that you should remember her name."

She neatly folded a bit of spinach salad onto her fork and placed it in her mouth, chewing thoughtfully. "I told you that when the time came, I'd remember the girl's name."

Caleb grimaced. "I'm not dating her, Mother."

"No? Oh. Well, I must have it completely wrong, then."

Of course, she didn't believe that. And he wasn't even going to attempt to convince her differently. To do so would only make her dig her heels in deeper.

"And your Mr. or Ms. Right?" he asked. "Was he or she in attendance last night?"

"Oh, heavens, no. Do you think I'd risk someone figuring anything out?"

"You mean like me?"

She smiled sweetly. "Exactly like you."

He pretended an interest in his fish, but the image of Bryna quietly gathering her things in his bedroom last night and leaving the penthouse burned into the back of his eyelids. Every time he blinked, there it was, taunting him, warning him, daring him to do something about the guilt he felt. The remorse that he'd hurt her.

Oh, not physically. Although what he'd done had played a role in establishing the distance he needed to put between the two of them. No. He'd shut himself off from her emotionally. Turning away when she might have snuggled against him. Rolling off as soon as he climaxed instead of lying still for long moments, reveling in the delicious sensations she brought him.

Without saying a word, he'd pounded a wedge between them that she'd at first been surprised by, then hurt.

And, shockingly, her being hurt had hurt him.

"So how do you two know each other?" his mother asked.

Caleb let his fork clatter to his plate and picked up the napkin in his lap. "I'm not seeing Bryna Metaxas, Mother. Leave it be."

"Mmm. That's why your face is so long. You didn't really think I wouldn't see it, did you? The whole room saw it, Caleb. You couldn't keep your eyes off her. And the same applied to her. You could virtually see the electricity that arced between the two of you."

He mutilated a bread roll with quick, irritated jerks.

"If you're not seeing her now, then you should be."

He quirked a sarcastic brow. "Oh? Suddenly you want grandchildren?"

She drew back as if his words had hit her like a blow.

Caleb immediately regretted the remark. There was no need to bring up the statement she'd made ten or so years ago about not wanting to be a grandmother. He hadn't paid much attention to it at the time. Had even put it down to her struggling with the date on the calendar, a showdown with her own mortality. He'd never truly thought she'd meant it.

Funny how he must have filed the throwaway comment away for use in this one moment.

"In fact," she said carefully, "I was thinking how nice it would be to have one or two grandchildren running around that I could spoil."

He stared at her.

She laughed. "I know. I told you that lately it's as if I don't know myself." She shook her head. "Five years ago I would have been horrified by the thought of you having children. Now…"

Caleb buttered one of the bread pieces. "Now…" he repeated.

"I think children would do you good. As well as me."

"And you've come to this conclusion how?"

She twisted her lips. "Sometimes…I don't know, Caleb. It seems as if we're both stuck in some sort of time warp. The image in the mirror changes, but it's a bit like Dorian Gray in that we don't. We go on as if we're going to be young and strong forever."

"So you want grandchildren for legacy reasons."

"No, no." She sighed and tapped her manicured nails against her wineglass before taking a sip. "I guess what I'm trying to say is that a change will do us both good."

Caleb chewed on his roll.

"I've been doing a lot of thinking lately, you know, since the doctor found that cyst on my breast."

He stopped chewing.

"No, no. Nothing like that. Some delayed menopausal reaction that should pass in a month or two. Nothing to worry about. At any rate, I'm being monitored."

He managed to swallow with help from his water.

He remembered his mother saying something about running into some minor health problem a month or so ago, but had no idea it had been a cyst or that it had been on her breast. He'd automatically assumed that it was something aesthetic, an unwanted mole on her arm or something of that nature.

He'd never sat down and considered that there would come a day in the distant or not too distant future that she wouldn't be there for him anymore.

And then he would be completely, utterly alone.

"Anyway, I've been thinking that maybe, all those years ago, I should have listened to my father. That I should have kept the identity of your father to myself. Married that man he tried to match me with and pass you off as his…"

Caleb gave up any pretense of eating altogether.

His mother had always been so strong, so adamant in her stance that the truth was always best. It was a moral code he'd learned early on, so when he was the bastard that he'd been called all his life, the other party couldn't say they weren't warned in advance.

"I don't know," she continued. "I just think that by naming your father publicly, and having him deny it, I placed us both in some sort of social limbo, as if both of us are waiting for something to happen that never will."

Caleb's gaze dropped to the table.

"I know we've talked about the possibility of obtaining a court-ordered DNA test to prove, once and for all, that Theodore Winstead was your biological father, but…" She folded her hands and worried her thumbs together. "What good would it do, really? We both know the truth. Does it really matter what the rest of the world thinks? In the end, does it really make any difference at all?"

Since the prospect of proving paternity had only to do with making his father's family publicly acknowledge his existence, he was surprised by his mother's thoughts.

"And even if we do ultimately decide to proceed… what will change? Will anyone look at either one of us any differently? Would doors that had been closed suddenly open?"

"You and I have never had a problem with closed doors."

She smiled. "No, we haven't, have we? We merely

forced them open." She reached for his hand where it rested next to his water glass. "Which is why I think we should just put this whole thing to bed. Now. Once and for all."

Caleb squinted at her. Whoever this man was she had met, he'd inspired changes in his mother that could never have come about through mere conversation.

He considered telling her about his legal attempts to force a DNA test and proof of paternity, but decided against it. Seeing the fresh light in her eyes, he thought the idea of putting the entire episode to bed, as she'd put it, was increasingly appealing.

"For the first time in my life," she said, "I want to move on. I wanted to forget about that chapter and start writing a new one from scratch."

"You want to forget about me?"

"No!"

Caleb grinned. "It was an attempt at a joke, Mother. I understand."

And, surprisingly, he did.

He'd lived for so long with the shadow of his dead, undeclared father eclipsing his own that he didn't know what it was like to take a breath without it there.

His mother squeezed his hand. "Give it some thought. If you'd like to proceed...of course we will."

A sharp pang sliced through his gut as he looked at her.

How much had she sacrificed for him? She'd borne a child on her own. A child his married father wouldn't publicly attest to. Had turned away suitors when he so much as opened his mouth. Had lived her life trying to heal the pain of his wounds, never considering her own.

She'd hurt when he'd hurt.

And now she didn't want to hurt anymore.

Could he take that away from her?

She began to withdraw her hand, but he held on to it. She blinked, her blue eyes questioning.

"Shall we hold a burial ceremony, I wonder?" he asked.

She held his gaze for a long moment, dampness making her eyes look extra bright.

"I think we just did, baby. I think we just did."

BRYNA SAT IN A CHAIR next to Caleb's secretary's desk clutching her briefcase tightly in both hands. After last night...

She forced air through her tight throat.

After last night she'd feared that Caleb would cancel his business appointment with her. Find some way out of it. Send her proposal back via courier with a terse note that would finish their business as well as personal ties.

He hadn't. But she wasn't altogether convinced that was a good thing.…

She swallowed hard, feeling much as she had that first day almost two weeks ago when she'd gathered the courage to make an appointment with him using her real name. She'd been surprised he'd taken it… and then waited a half hour after the time they were to meet only to be told that he wasn't interested in reviewing any ideas from her.

Then she'd changed his mind.

Where just yesterday she might have looked back fondly on the moment, now she knew only fear.

Fear of what she'd see in his eyes when she gazed at him.

Fear of what she might say to erase the look.

Fear of what she might do to coax the one she wanted back.

The secretary picked up the telephone extension and then quietly put it back down.

"He'll see you now, Miss Metaxas."

Bryna got to her feet, feeling as if her knees were suddenly as substantial as the marmalade she'd tried to choke down along with toast for breakfast. She offered up her thanks and a weak smile to the secretary and then crossed to the door, switching her briefcase from her right to her left hand and turning the knob.

He stood at the windows, his back to her.

She knew relief.

"Thank you for not canceling," she said, her voice sounding far more confident than she felt.

She moved to the table and opened her briefcase, pulling out the sheath of papers and the pad she'd brought along.

She heard him turn from the window, but ordered herself not to look up. Not to gaze into his face.

"I'm sorry," he said, his voice so cold that the hair on her arms stood on end. "But I'm going to have to put an end to this now...."

16

BRYNA FELT AS IF the bottom had been cut out of her stomach.

She straightened, fastened a smile to her mouth, then turned to face Caleb.

"I'm sorry?" she said.

He didn't move. Didn't say anything. Merely stood looking at her as if she were an adversary, and not an equal one at that.

She was reminded again of their first meeting. Except then she'd glimpsed attraction in his eyes, sexual challenge. Now...now she saw nothing but distance.

"This proposal isn't viable," he said.

Bryna crossed her arms, searching wildly within for the weapon she needed to pierce his armor. "In which way?"

"In every way."

What did he expect her to do? Turn tail and run?

She felt her spine strengthen. Well, then, he was in for a big disappointment.

"You're going to have to do better than that. I want details."

Was that a quirk of a brow? An upward twitch of the left side of his mouth?

He slowly walked past her. For a moment, she was afraid he was going to go to the door and open it, showing her the way out. She held her breath, battling against the tears that stung the back of her eyes.

Instead, he took something off his desktop and walked to the table, placing the sheath of papers next to hers. He was so near, she could smell the scent of his lime aftershave. It was all she could do not to breath it in, revel in the intimate scent, because she didn't know if she ever would again.

"First, the numbers don't add up," he said, pointing to a column.

Bryna squinted at him. Was he really talking details?

"So…when you said the proposal wasn't viable, you meant as is," she said carefully. "Which means you're willing to hammer out something together."

This close, she could make out the golden specks in his rich brown eyes. "Are you going to focus on what I'm saying?"

"Oh, I'm hearing every word you're saying. Even the silent words in between those words."

He drew up again.

She couldn't help noticing that he appeared to be

steeling himself as much as she was attempting to do against him.

Which was odd. Why would he want to do that?

She forced her gaze away from his, instead pulling a chair out and taking a seat at the table. She pushed her papers aside and pulled his forward, considering the columns he'd pointed to.

"The numbers don't work because you were looking at the wrong numbers," she said simply.

She gave him back his papers and riffled through her own.

"If you take a look here, the end result makes perfect sense."

He didn't move for a long moment. She looked over her shoulder to find his gaze on the back of her neck, left bare by her upswept style. She shivered for an altogether different reason than a few moments ago. His expression was one of those that made her seek out and identify every flat surface in the room. Anything they could use to indulge the incredible attraction that existed between them.

He met her gaze and she saw the same confusion and sizzling chaos that had been there since the beginning.

Finally, he cleared his throat and took a chair a couple up from hers.

Bryna was disappointed by his obvious attempt at physical as well as emotional distance but was determined not to show it. She was here for business. To save Metaxas Limited. To save Earnest.

The rest...well, the rest would have to wait.

He reviewed her papers. "I see what you mean."

They went back and forth, with Bryna presenting him with the counterarguments she had prepared, and Caleb not giving an inch in any point.

The intercom buzzed.

Bryna looked at her watch, surprised that over an hour had passed as Caleb rose to pick up the extension on his desk.

"Yes...I see. Thank you."

They were nowhere near a compromise, the spot that would allow him to take the proposal and approach potential investors on behalf of Metaxas Limited. But Bryna got the distinct impression that the meeting was over.

"My one o'clock is here," he said simply.

Bryna nodded, swallowing past the lump in her throat as she separated her files from his.

"But he can wait."

She jerked to look up at him.

He sighed and walked away from her, then stopped and leaned against a wingback chair. He crossed his arms.

"You have a good proposal here, Bryna...but I'm not sure it's something I can proceed with."

"And the reason for that..."

He ran his hand over his face, surprising her with the exasperated move. "There are many...but the top one is that Metaxas doesn't have enough invested in the proposal."

She got to her feet and faced him, leaning her arm against the back of the table chair. "We have over a year invested in the project. Thirty people contracted and on the payroll working nonstop to make this thing happen."

"I'm talking financially."

"What? Like a monetary investment beyond what I've already proven?"

He nodded. "I don't have to tell you that this is a hard economic environment. You couldn't sell a glass of water to a man crossing the desert." He slid one of his hands into the pocket of his slacks. "Any potential investors will want to know that your company stands to lose as much as they will."

She frowned.

"It's the only thing that will prove that Metaxas Limited is in this for the long haul, not just looking for capital on an iffy venture that may not come to fruition, leaving the investor out and Metaxas Limited untouched financially."

"We have a great deal invested in this project."

"But do you have cash resources?"

"If we had cash resources, we wouldn't need to find a partner."

"But without an even investment, no one's going to sign on, Bryna. Not in this tough environment."

He walked to the table and gathered his own files, stacking them up neatly and moving them to the top of his desk.

"Until you can come up with solid resources

outside that which you've already shown me, I'm afraid there's nowhere for us to go from here."

"Define solid."

"A good seven figures."

"That's outrageous! If we had access to that kind of cash—"

He raised a hand. "You asked."

A sense of doom settled into the pit of her bottomless stomach. She methodically slid her materials into her briefcase.

What scared her even more was the possibility that if she walked out that door without the promise of future discussions, she might never see him again.

"What if I were to come up with those resources?" she asked suddenly.

He narrowed his eyes. "I think it's time you let your cousins in on what you're doing, Bryna."

"I asked you a question."

"Are you talking personally?"

"I'm talking resources. Who cares where they come from?"

He opened his mouth, then closed it again. She suspected he was about to say, "I care." Then changed his mind.

She mentally calculated what she had in her personal accounts. Outside of paying for her small apartment in a quaint section of Seattle, she'd barely touched her inheritance. That combined with the many investments she'd made and savings from her salary, could easily amount to…

"How about mid-six figures," she asked. "Would that be enough to move forward?"

He didn't say anything for a long moment. Merely stood considering her.

She wished she could climb into his head. See the thoughts there. Know what he was thinking. More, learn what he was feeling.

"It would be a start."

"I asked if it's enough to move forward. For you to begin approaching potential investors? To put this deal together? To make it happen?"

The silence of the room seemed to emphasize the hard thud of her heartbeat.

"Yes," he said.

Bryna felt a relief so complete she nearly sat back down in the chair.

Instead, she finished packing her briefcase, snapped it closed and then strode toward the door.

"I'll have the funds together by the end of the working day."

"Bryna?"

She didn't respond. She merely continued out the door and then down the hall, not stopping until she reached the elevators. It was only when the doors whooshed shut that she finally allowed herself to exhale.

And began to hope that this was going to work out...

LATER THAT DAY, Bryna let herself into her apartment, all too aware of its silence. At the Metaxas estate in Earnest, there was always some sort of sound coming from inside the house. Whether it was the housekeeper sweeping one of the rooms, Ari getting something to eat in the kitchen, Troy talking on the phone in his home office, there was always movement, activity.

She found it ironic that while she had purchased the Seattle apartment for peace, now she wanted anything but.

She dropped her briefcase onto the hall table and then took her pumps off one by one, leaving them where they lay against the creamy beige marble tile. She switched on lights as she went, checked the automatic thermostat and then turned on the television, immediately soothed by the sound of a local anchor reporting the news.

After putting on the single-cup coffeemaker to brew in the kitchen, she went into the living room and collapsed onto the overstuffed couch covered with pale green vines and roses, tucking her feet under her even as she shrugged out of her suit jacket.

It was done.

As promised, she'd had her bank put her assets together and managed to squeeze out the amount promised to Caleb. A couple of phone calls later and the resources were deposited into a holding account, and Caleb had guaranteed that he'd have some news—good or bad remained to be seen—for her by next week.

Bryna sighed and leaned her head against her

hand. A tendril of hair had escaped her bun. She reached back and pulled out the pins, her scalp tingling as her hair dropped around her shoulders.

She wasn't sure what was bothering her. She'd accomplished what she'd set out to do—Caleb had agreed to actively solicit an investor in Metaxas Limited's plans. She should be celebrating.

Instead, she felt like doing anything but.

She sighed again and then pushed herself up from the sofa.

"Oh, stop it already. You knew the guy wasn't forever material. So what if he was the best you ever had?" She stomped in her bare feet toward the kitchen and the cup of coffee that waited there, the aroma filling the two-bedroom apartment. "At least you got it. You should be thanking the gods for at least that much."

The problem was how did you go forward knowing that the best you would ever achieve lay in your past?

She added a dollop of cream to the coffee, wrinkled her nose at the sip she took and then added a teaspoon and then another of sugar.

The buzz announcing that someone wanted building access at the front door sounded. She nearly spilled the hot liquid as she was taking another testing sip.

Caleb...

Her heart skipped a beat. She put the cup down and hurried to the hall to press the intercom button.

"Yes?" she said.

"Bryna?"

Ari.

She collapsed against the wall, not realizing how much she'd wanted it to be Caleb until she'd discovered it wasn't him.

_17_

"Is THAT ANY WAY to welcome your long-lost cousin?" Ari asked, entering her apartment as she held the door open.

"You're neither long nor lost, whatever that means," she said as she closed the door, but not until after a quick peek into the hall. She wasn't sure what she'd hoped to find. Caleb hiding in the shadows, perhaps?

The thought actually made her shudder. Especially in light of the other night and the liberties he'd requested…and that she'd offered up without objection.

"What are you doing in Seattle?" she asked Ari, following him into the kitchen.

He put down the bags he held on the counter and took a sip from her coffee cup. "Damn. How can you drink this stuff?"

"It's easy. I put my lips to the cup and swallow."

He dumped the contents down the drain, much to her despair.

"Hey! I was drinking that."

He opened one of the bags and took out a blue disposable cup with a Greek key design lining the rim. "Try this."

She moved to get the cream from the refrigerator and he blocked her.

"As is first. Then you can alter it…if you still want to."

Bryna popped off the top, sniffed the liquid and then took a slow sip. Okay, so it was good. And it didn't need a single thing added. In fact, cream or sugar would probably mask its deep, rich taste, which would be a shame.

Ari was grinning. "Good, huh?"

Bryna stepped to the counter and peered into the other bags he'd brought. "What else you got?"

He moved them out of range. "Nope. This is not how this works." He grasped her shoulders and steered her toward the butcher-block kitchen table. "You sit. I serve."

Bryna obeyed, if only because she didn't have the energy just then to fight him. Not that it would do her any good, anyway. Ari somehow always got what he wanted.

She sat in a kitchen chair, bending one of her feet under her, and watched as her cousin took two plates from the cupboard. Then he carefully positioned himself so that he blocked her view, keeping her from seeing what he was doing. He took another plate out, and then finally turned and put all three on the table.

"Voilà!" he said.

Bryna looked down at the dishes filled with Greek delicacies, from *dolmades*—stuffed grape leaves—and tzatziki to moussaka and grilled octopus. Just smelling the aromas wafting off the plates was enough to make her mouth water.

She held her hand palm up.

"What?" Ari asked.

"Fork?"

"Oh!" He took two forks from a drawer and then joined her at the table. "Dig in. Every last thing here is as great as it looks."

Bryna did exactly that, humming her approval as she went.

Despite the Metaxas family being Greek-American, it was rare that they actually dined on traditional Greek food. As the octopus melted against her tongue, she wondered why exactly that was. Her mother had always kept a Greek kitchen. And she understood that her aunt, Ari's mother, had, too.

Why, then, was it rare that Greek food was served at home? And when was the last time she'd actually cooked anything remotely Greek?

She frowned. She was having a hard time remembering when she'd actually cooked, period.

Before she knew it, she'd devoured everything on the plates, with a little help from Ari. She hadn't even realized she was hungry. Now she felt stuffed beyond comfort.

"Where'd you get this?" she asked. "Is there a new Greek restaurant here in town I don't know about?"

Ari sat back and grinned that knowing grin of his.

Oh, God.

Bryna made a face. "Elena made this."

"Yep. She's trying out family recipes, testing what she wants to offer on the menu when she opens the restaurant for dinner next week."

Bryna collected the plates, ran them under the faucet and then loaded them into the dishwasher. "She has a Greek place?"

"No. A general restaurant. That's why she needs to pick and choose what Greek dishes she can offer alongside the typical American fare."

"Shame. She should open a Greek place. Everything was delicious."

The compliment wasn't difficult to offer up. The food was great. No matter who had made it.

Ari sat back in his chair. "Don't put any ideas into her head. I'm having a difficult time as it is trying to convince her that she doesn't need to be working so hard. Especially right now."

Bryna poured the cup of coffee he'd brought into two mugs and handed him one. "I thought the restaurant was already open."

"It is. She started with breakfast. And now offers

lunch. But things are going so well, she'd like to open for dinner next week."

She leaned against the counter. "That should put a crimp in your love life."

Ari's long-suffering sigh made her smile. "Tell me about it."

She tapped her fingernails against the cup. "So what happens to this place if she buys the Quality Diner in Earnest?"

He got to his feet and budged her over. She hadn't realized he'd left anything on the counter. "Her mother has been working with her since she reopened and her brother has recently come in. They all worked at the restaurant before when her father ran it, so it's my guess she'll be leaving the restaurant to them, so to speak."

"So the place isn't hers?"

"Technically, no. Her mother inherited it."

Bryna nodded.

"Now for dessert," he said, holding out a plate.

Her groan filled the entire apartment. She didn't think she could possibly swallow another bite of anything...until she got a gander of what the plate held.

"Oh, God! I don't know how long it's been since I've had *sokolatina!*" She eyed the generous piece of chocolate torte. "And baklava!"

She forked a bite of each into her mouth one after another while Ari looked on in amusement.

"Buy...her...that...diner...now!" she told him.

Ari's smile slipped.

"Well, that's the problem."

Bryna didn't respond right away. She was too busy pigging out on the sweets.

Eventually she asked, "But I thought she was interested in buying The Quality."

"She is. With the emphasis on *she*."

Bryna's chewing slowed. "I don't understand."

"I don't either. But there you have it. She wants to be the one to buy the diner. Not me."

Finally Bryna's stomach refused to accept another bite.

How long had it been since she'd eaten that much? God, even her skirt suddenly felt tight.

She sighed, staring longingly at the half-eaten contents of the plate. Then she forced herself to put the plate down, cheering herself up with the fact that it would still be there for her later.

Ari picked up her fork and made to take a bite.

"Touch that, lose a limb." She took the fork out of his hand and put it in the sink and then moved to put the plate in the refrigerator, out of reach.

His chuckle warmed the room at the same time as the buzzer rang for the second time that night.

Ari raised a brow. "Expecting company?"

It took Bryna a moment to force air through the tight passage of her throat. "No," she fairly croaked.

"Well, expected or not, it looks like you've got some."

He began walking toward the door.

"Thanks so much for coming by," she said, wishing there were an easier way to do this. Hand him his coat, his hat, something, anything other than practically snatching the coffee cup from his hands and shoving him through the door.

"Okay. So you might not be expecting company, but I'm getting the impression that you were hoping for it."

Bryna glared at him as the buzzer rang again.

"Thanks for dinner, Ari." She kissed him on the cheek and reached around him to push the buzzer even as she opened the door and shoved him out. "I'll see you at home on Sunday."

"Fine. I can take a hint. But you do realize that I'm going to see who this mystery visitor is, don't you? I think I just might have to introduce myself to him."

Bryna's lungs froze as the man in question appeared in the hall behind her cousin.

"No need," Caleb said. "We've already met...."

18

IT WAS OBVIOUS that Caleb hadn't expected to run into Ari at her place. Just as obvious was that he didn't care what his one-time adversary thought. But Bryna did.

She'd always known that there would be problems if her cousins discovered she was seeing Manolis Philippidis's right-hand man. But it was a worry that had vanished earlier that day when she'd stood face-to-face with Caleb in his office and realized that whatever they had shared for so brief a time was over.

Or so she'd thought.

Ari stood staring at the other man, his face frozen in surprise.

"Ari," Caleb said quietly, extending his hand.

Her cousin glanced at him, his outstretched hand, and then at Bryna, obviously trying to piece everything together.

"Come on in, Caleb," Bryna said, her heart beating an erratic rhythm in her chest. A condition caused as much by Caleb's appearance as Ari's accidental discovery.

She quickly kissed her cousin on the cheek. "Talk to you later, Ari. Good night."

And just like that, Caleb was inside the apartment and the door was closed on her cousin, Caleb's hand left untouched.

For long moments they stood silently. She heard Ari's quiet curses as he finally started to descend the stairs.

Caleb cleared his throat as Bryna leaned against the door and closed her eyes.

Please just let him leave in peace, she prayed.

"I hope I didn't cause any problems," Caleb said.

The buzzer sounded and she jumped, her nerves raw.

She bit her bottom lip and then pressed the intercom button. "What do you want, Ari?"

"I want to know what he's doing here."

She took a deep breath. "I don't think this is the time to have this discussion."

Silence. She let go of the button.

The buzzer sounded again.

"Good night, Ari," she said insistently.

"Bryn…if you need anything…"

She turned so that Caleb couldn't see her face, touched by the concern in her cousin's voice, no matter how irritating he was being at that particular moment. "I know where to find you," she whispered. "Drive carefully."

She didn't realize she was still holding the button until Caleb cleared his throat again.

She rubbed her palm against her skirt and turned to face a man she had hoped to see again, but never expected to see in her apartment. Every bite she'd eaten a short time ago sat in her stomach like a pile of pebbles. She searched his face, but was unable to discern what he might be thinking. His demeanor differed very little from what she'd encountered in his office earlier…yet here he was. Standing in her apartment.

She squinted at him. "What are you doing here, Caleb?"

WHAT WAS HE DOING THERE, indeed. Now, that was a good question.

The last place he'd expected to find himself tonight was at Bryna's place. He usually made it a point to keep the ball in his court, in his penthouse, everything going by his rules.

Now…

He looked around the small but smart apartment that undoubtedly had a great view of the city when the curtains were open. Unlike his place, this one spoke of comfort and accessibility. Yes, there was a stereo and a television, but neither was the focus like they were at his home. Instead, two couches and two chairs were positioned around a large, rustic communal coffee table filled with flowers. Floor-to-ceiling bookcases were stuffed with titles ranging from the classics to nonfiction. Magazines and newspapers were stacked on the floor next to one of the couches. Plants were everywhere, as were photographs, both black-and-white prints and color, framed and covering every available surface, faces smiling into the camera lens. There didn't seem to be space for one more thing, yet everything appeared perfectly in place.

Except for him.

He looked back at Bryna, who was still waiting for him to answer.

Her blouse was wrinkled, her feet bare, her hair tousled. And she couldn't have looked more beautiful if she'd tried.

"I don't know," he found himself answering honestly.

With anyone else, he might have offered up an excuse. Perhaps even turned the question on the occupant, inferring from the inquiry that he wasn't welcome in order to elicit a guilt-ridden response. But they'd moved beyond that, hadn't they? Well beyond that.

But since this territory was uncharted for him, he didn't know on what part of the map he stood, much less where he should go from there.

All he knew was that he wanted to kiss her with an intensity that made his groin ache.

He drew closer to her. She moved back, her eyes wide in her face.

"I don't—"

He trapped her objection between his mouth and hers. A silent groan surged upward in his throat. She tasted of honey and coffee and something one hundred percent pure Bryna.

Caleb didn't know what it was about this one woman that brought him to his knees where others had failed. She was smart. She was sexy as hell. But she was as different from him as sunshine was to rain.

Why, then, couldn't he stop thinking about her? Stop wanting her? No matter how many times he kissed her. How many times they had sex. He wanted more. And even more after that.

His hands roamed freely over her hot body even as he pressed himself against her soft belly. The wall supported her from behind as she plunged her fingers into his hair and kissed him back with the same passion that filled him.

Strangely, even now he felt conflicted. He wanted to take her right then, right there. But rather than finding relief in the overpowering emotion, he instead felt…almost rueful somehow.

He thrust his hand between her knees, marveling at the softness of her skin even as he budged her skirt upward. She automatically spread her thighs, gasping as his fingertips met with the damp crotch of her panties.

She was always ready for him. No matter when he reached for her, she was there, waiting. No matter what storm raged, inside or out, she clutched him as tightly as he held her.

Christ, she felt so good. Stroking her like this, hearing her soft sounds, he wanted for nothing else in the world.

Yet he wanted for everything.

With a quick yank, he tore her panties off. When it appeared she might object, he slid two fingers down the dripping channel created by her swollen flesh, quickly entering her, not stopping until her slick muscles trembled around him.

He kissed her deeply again, his breathing hard, his heart beating even harder. Damn it, he wanted to possess her. To bring her to her knees the same way she had so effortlessly done to him. He undid the catch on his slacks and reached in for his throbbing erection. There was no time for condom searching. He wanted her now. And he needed to know that she needed him the same way.

He grasped her hips and lifted her until her calves went around his thighs. Then he entered her in one long stroke, not stopping until he was in to the hilt.

Bryna's nails bit into his shoulders through his jacket and shirt, her eyes hooded, her mouth open in a silent *oh*. He thrust again, reaching for an even deeper meeting. Then again, one hand supporting her peach-shaped ass from behind, the other braced against the wall.

Her tight muscles convulsed around him.

Caleb set his back teeth, determined not to follow. He wanted this to last. Wanted to extend the moment for as long as he could. Because it was only in moments like these, when he was joined with her, that he felt whole. That he felt normal. Like the world made sense in some sort of inexplicable way.

His hips bucked forward and he groaned, his body issuing urgent orders all its own....

BRYNA'S HEART POUNDED so hard she was afraid it might break through the wall of her chest. Chaotic emotions raged through her. When she was in Caleb's arms, felt him inside her, it was easy to forget the rest. But now...now the reality of their situation hit her full force, crowding out everything but confusion and pain.

She slowly slid to stand on her feet and splayed her hands against his chest. She ordered herself to push him away, but instead reveled in the feel of the wall of muscle beneath his shirt, the sound of his ragged breathing filling her ear where his face was still buried in her hair.

Finally she gathered her wits about her and forced him away.

Caleb looked everywhere but into her face as he tucked his still-hard penis back into his slacks and refastened them.

"I...don't understand...." she whispered, feeling ridiculously close to tears.

He still didn't look at her. "I'm sorry. I didn't mean for that to happen."

She bit hard on her bottom lip. "What?" The word came out barely audible. "Are you really apologizing for…"

For what? Having sex with her? Because it hadn't been making love. Caleb had made it very clear that he held no emotion for her whatsoever beyond human need.

He finally met her gaze. She caught her breath. Or did he feel more than he was willing to admit?

She raised her hand as if to ward him off. "Whatever…this…is, Caleb. I don't want it."

He remained silent, watching her.

She swallowed hard against the emotion threatening to choke her. "What we met…it was a mutual thing. Attraction. I wanted you. You wanted me. Simple enough…"

She slid out from between him and the wall and stepped into the living room, putting much needed space between him and her.

"At least that's how it started.…"

His eyes hardened and she stared at him.

"But somewhere down the line…well, it grew into more for me." Her voice cracked on the last word. "I think…no, I know I began falling in love with you.…"

He looked away. She stormed forward.

"Don't you dare pretend like you don't hear me."

The floor was cold beneath her feet.

"Don't act like you don't know. I know you know. Because you were feeling the same thing...."

And she did know that. Her knee-jerk reaction to his coldness had blocked out her own sense of the situation, of what had been developing between the two of them, but now...now she understood he felt more, far more, for her than he was letting on.

"Look...I'm guessing there's a good reason why you won't...can't open yourself up to me." A single tear rolled hotly down her cheek. "But this...what just happened...what occurred the other night...it stops here."

She steeled herself. Not against him. But against herself.

"I can't deal with what I'm feeling and your hang-ups at the same time."

They stood staring at each other for what seemed like an eternity. Bryna felt incapable of breathing. Incapable of moving.

Finally he dropped his gaze and nodded.

Bryna knew a pinprick of anticipation.

"I understand," he said simply. When he lifted his head again, the coldness was back in his eyes. "But you're wrong. I don't love you, Bryna."

The pinprick of optimism morphed into a stab in the heart.

"I don't know what love is."

Then he turned and let himself out of the apartment, quietly closing the door and any hope for the future behind him....

19

THE FOLLOWING NIGHT Caleb stood in front of his penthouse window watching rain stream down the smooth glass like liquid beads. The past day had passed in a blur of meetings and phone calls…and he was having a hard time recalling exactly what had been said.

"Sir?"

He turned toward Lionel, his houseman.

"I've put the remainder of your dinner in the refrigerator should you wish to finish it later."

He nodded, thankful for Lionel's unwavering discretion. In truth, he hadn't eaten a bite of the meal. "Thank you. That will be all."

"Very good, sir. Good evening."

"Good evening."

He barely heard the other man make preparations to leave the penthouse for the night and return to his own apartment on a lower floor. He'd already turned back toward the windows, his mind virtually paralyzed, his body strangely numb.

He thought about calling one of the many names of friendly females in what amounted to his little black book. Preferably someone who would take his mind off Bryna, but wouldn't want anything beyond tonight.

A booty call.

He smiled slightly at the reference, a moment that was gone as quickly as it appeared.

He slid his hands into his pockets. No music played. No drink waited. He had no plans. And he couldn't seem to bring himself to change one thing. It was as if a switch had been toggled, holding him in place. Forcing him to look at something he was missing.

But he saw nothing.

Finally he turned away from the window and went to the foyer closet, taking his coat out. He considered calling his driver James to take him somewhere. But he didn't know where he'd go. Instead, he shrugged into his overcoat, bypassed an umbrella and took the elevator down to the lobby, barely acknowledging the front doorman as he hurried to open the door for him.

He stopped in the middle of the sidewalk, closed his eyes and tilted his face up toward the sky. Raindrops, cool and steady, fell down his skin. For a moment, one sweet moment, he was offered relief from his thoughts and he grabbed at it, only to lose it the instant he did.

"Mr. Payne?"

He didn't acknowledge the doorman.

"Is everything all right, sir?"

Caleb took a deep breath, opened his eyes and glanced in his general direction. "Fine. Everything's fine."

He began walking. He wasn't sure where. He just didn't want to be interrupted again.

Seattle's streets were dark and oily, lights reflecting off the wet surfaces. Within five minutes, he was soaked to the bone, but he couldn't bring himself to care.

Imprinted on his mind was the image of Bryna's face the last time he'd seen her. The tortured expression she'd worn.

Anger he could deal with. And was usually what he encountered when a relationship reached its natural conclusion. But he'd never gotten such sadness.

He smoothed his wet hair back from his forehead several times. What had he been thinking when he'd taken her into his bed? When he'd wrongly assumed that Bryna Metaxas could be an intriguing diversion between more suitable dates?

He'd never meant to hurt her.

He winced.

What was he saying? He'd never cared one iota if he'd hurt anyone before. Why the guilty conscience now?

She was so young. More than chronologically. While she was as smart as anyone he'd come across, he had at least a decade's life experience on her.

And that was it, wasn't it? She'd mistaken great sex for love.

An honest mistake, to be sure. Because the sex had been phenomenal. In fact, he couldn't remember a time when he'd enjoyed a woman's body more. But sex was just sex. It wasn't a relationship.

His jaw tensed. If that's what he believed, then why in the hell was he out walking in the goddamn rain on a Friday night by himself with no destination in mind?

BY LATE SATURDAY AFTERNOON, Bryna was concerned her family was on the verge of staging an intervention. In a part of her brain that still worked, she figured she wouldn't blame them if they did. After Caleb had left her Thursday, she'd paced her apartment for a couple of hours and then finally locked the place up and headed to Earnest and home, where she'd promptly shut herself into her bedroom and hadn't ventured out since.

Ari, Troy and her uncle had all made appearances at the door, with Ari even making it as far as the bed.

She lay under those same covers now, blocking out the early-evening sunlight that burst through the clouds, slanting in her windows. She sniffed. Then sniffed again. Then quickly folded the covers back.

She needed a shower something terrible. But she couldn't bring herself to leave the bed for more than the necessary runs to her connected bathroom.

She wasn't physically ill. At least not with anything that a doctor could help her with. No, no antibiotic or medication could help her with what she was suffering through. Not unless they'd discovered a magical elixir that would help heal her broken heart.

She eyed the untouched food tray on her bedside table. She couldn't remember anyone bringing it, but like clockwork, one was delivered three times a day. Ari? Likely. She couldn't imagine Troy doing it. Then again, the men in her life seemed to be surprising her a lot lately.

Especially Caleb.

The problem was that Caleb wasn't really in her life, was he? Had never been. To him, she'd been nothing more interesting than an amusement park ride he could leave behind when he became bored in search of the next one.

She grimaced. Now, there was analogy for you. She was a roller coaster. Or at the very least, she felt like she was riding one. And had just come to the end without hope of ever mounting it again.

Mounting it. Ugh.

From out of the blue, a sob rose in her throat and again she was crying.

Okay, even she was getting tired of this. So he'd hurt her. She'd known the dangers going in. A man like Caleb Payne wasn't one to be thrown by simple emotion. And, after all, he had that "love 'em and leave 'em" reputation to live up to. Plus his name.

Payne. Pain.

It couldn't have been clearer had it been tattooed across his handsome forehead.

But that didn't make it any easier to take.

She reached for the box of tissues next to her bed only to find it empty. She looked around for a semi-used one, only to find them littering the floor on either side of her bed. She stared at the linen napkin on the food tray and pulled it out from under the silverware, loudly blowing her nose into the starchy fabric.

She needed to go on a tissue run.

Stripping back the covers, she padded barefoot to the bathroom. Even the toilet paper roll was empty. And there wasn't an extra under the sink.

Great.

She went back into her bedroom and pulled her robe on. She couldn't find her slippers so she left them as she went in search of more tissue.

"...that son of a bitch doesn't know who he's messing with." She heard Troy's voice as she neared the kitchen. "If this is some kind of game Philippidis has arranged, I swear—"

"It didn't look like a game to me," Ari said. "I mean, I couldn't tell you exactly what was going on between the two of them, but I can assure you that Bryna is a smart girl. She would never allow someone like Caleb Payne to hurt her."

Troy snorted. "Oh, yeah? Then why has she been locked inside her room for two days straight crying her heart out? I'm going to kill him."

Bryna stood in the doorway looking at her cousins, who sat on stools at the kitchen island. Her uncle was drinking a cup of coffee on the other side, while Elena was loading the dishwasher.

Bryna squinted at them, her heart beating an impossible rhythm in her chest.

It was one thing to deal with all this on her own. Adding her cousin's concerns to the mix was almost more than she could bear.

Her throat refused her voice. She turned on her heel to go back upstairs, remembered she'd come for a reason, and then stalked to the supply closet and grabbed a box of tissues and a roll of toilet paper. Then she stalked back through the room, the path in front of her blurry.

"Bryna, wait," Elena called.

She kept going, not stopping until after she'd slammed her bedroom door and run for her bed, once again burying herself under the covers....

BRYNA COULDN'T BE SURE how long she'd slept. All she knew was that when she opened her eyes sometime later, the sun had set...and Elena was walking into her bedroom with a fresh food tray.

She moved to cover her face with the blankets, then decided differently and left them where they were.

She did, however, close her eyes, deciding to act like she was still asleep.

She listened as Elena replaced the tray with the fresh one. She waited to hear the door close after her.

"I know you're awake," Elena said instead.

Bryna made a face. "You must be psychic."

Elena laughed quietly and then Bryna felt her weight on the large bed. She opened one eye, peering at the other woman.

"Did the guys put you up to this?" she asked.

Elena's eyes widened. "The guys…? Oh. No."

She didn't say anything more.

Bryna stared at her openly now. Couldn't she tell that she didn't want company? A closed bedroom door should certainly be a clear sign that she wanted some privacy, if not the covers over her face?

Elena smiled awkwardly then plucked at the hem of her shirt. "Look, Bryna, I know you don't care for me much."

Definitely psychic.

"I'm not entirely certain why, but that doesn't matter. Not this minute. We can work all that out later."

Why not now?

Bryna grimaced at her silent side of the conversation.

"But seeing you like this…in bed, shutting out the world…well, reminds me of what I went through such a short time ago."

What she was experiencing was nothing like what had happened between Elena and Ari, Bryna silently maintained.

Her hope was that if she remained quiet, the other woman would finally get up and leave.

"I know you probably don't think it does, but..." She tucked a strand of hair that had escaped her ponytail behind her ear. Was her hand shaking, or was Bryna imagining things? Elena laughed thinly. "It isn't easy to one moment think you have the world all figured out, then the next be thrown into another reality by what amounts to little more than a sucker punch to the chest."

Bryna sucked her lips into her mouth; the description nailed her own feelings dead on.

"Add on top of that the fact that your family is completely against your relationship and...well, you have a clear recipe for disaster."

"Your family was against you being with Ari?" Bryna found herself asking.

Elena gaped at her. "Are you kidding me? My...affair with him ruined everything they'd ever wanted." Her gaze fell to where she rubbed her palms against the legs of her jeans. "I didn't figure out until sometime later that it wasn't what they wanted for me, but rather what they needed for themselves."

"I don't understand...."

Elena raised a hand and waved it. "That doesn't matter now. None of it does. Although my mother still occasionally insists that Manolis Philippidis will take me back."

"Even though you're pregnant with Ari's child?"

"That's usually my response. But mostly I just ignore her because her comments typically come after a long shift spent at the restaurant when she's been on her feet all day."

Bryna folded the blankets down even farther. "I don't understand. I mean you could marry Ari now, move in here, and have enough money to take care of your family, too. Why don't you do it? I know Ari wants that."

Elena smiled sadly and her hand went to her still-flat belly, a seemingly unconscious move that touched Bryna. "Because I don't want to make the same mistake twice. This time I want to go into my marriage with my own independent means. I want to pursue my own interests. And I don't ever want Ari or anyone else to think that I'm marrying him only for the money."

"And Philippidis? Weren't you going to marry him just for the money?"

Elena's expression was rueful. "See. That's exactly the reason why I don't run off to the county judge's today, this instant, and marry the man I love with all my heart. Because everyone questions and probably will always question what my motivations were in agreeing to be Philippidis's wife."

"An honest reaction."

"Perhaps. But I would never consider marrying

anyone for money." She smiled. "Which brings me around to the point I came in here to make."

"I thought you'd come in here to bug me."

She laughed. "If it chases you out of your bed, then it would be just as effective."

By now Bryna was actually sitting up, the covers bunched around her crossed legs as she considered the other woman.

"You see, Manolis had been a friend of our family for as long as I can remember. He and my father came over here from Greece at around the same time. He was more like an uncle to me than anything. And then my father died and…"

She trailed off and Bryna sat waiting patiently.

"And, well, Manolis was like an angel to me and my family. Before I knew what was happening, we'd begun dating. And when he asked me to marry him, I saw no reason why I shouldn't…"

Bryna wanted to ask questions, but Elena was in her own world now.

"Until I met Ari. Until I understood…love."

"You didn't love Manolis?"

Elena half smiled. "I thought I did. I was convinced I did. But what Ari inspired in me…" She sighed wistfully. "Well, I knew immediately that while I might love Manolis—then, anyway—I wasn't in love with him. Not with the soul-stirring passion that I love Ari."

"And you knew that immediately?"

"Yes."

Bryna nodded.

"So I guess what I'm trying to say, Bryna, is that you shouldn't let anyone else influence how you feel about someone." She reached out and took Bryna's hand where it rested against her knee, already resembling the mother she would soon be. "You can't choose who you love no sooner than you can change the color of the sky."

Bryna stared at her, speechless.

"What you can choose, however, is how that love will manifest itself."

"I don't understand."

"I didn't either. At least not until Ari refused to let me go…" She sighed. "What I mean is, this… whatever you're feeling for Caleb Payne? It's up to you to decide what to do with it. You can either go the rest of your life knowing that you had that once-in-a-lifetime love within your grasp and let it get away… or you can grab it tightly with both hands and refuse to let it go. Because to do so would be a sin against the gods of the highest order."

Bryna held her breath, wanting to tell her that the choice wasn't hers. That Caleb had made the decision for both of them. But she couldn't seem to force the words from her throat.

Instead, she suddenly threw her arms around Elena and held her close. "Thank you," she whispered into the shocked woman's ear.

"Don't mention it. We Metaxas women are few. We should stick together, don't you think?"

Bryna leaned back and looked into her smiling eyes. "I do now...."

20

"OKAY, NOW I'm really starting to worry about you," Phoebe Payne said across the table from Caleb over Sunday brunch.

He looked at her. So he'd barely said a word. That wasn't so unusual. Especially lately. Really, he shouldn't have come to the upscale restaurant. But the thought of staying in that empty apartment for one more minute alone had been even less appealing.

"Are you going to tell me what's going on?" his mother asked. "Or am I going to have to get up and leave you to eat alone?"

Caleb tensed, his chaotic emotions coalescing briefly in anger. "Do what you have to."

Phoebe leaned forward, not about to back down on this one. "Don't think that I won't," she threatened.

This was her last day in town. Later in the evening she was catching a red-eye back to New York. If he allowed her to stay upset with him now, he knew he was in for months of strained relations.

He grasped the napkin in his lap with his right hand, wringing it tightly. "Actually, I do have a question for you…" he began, unsure what he was going to say or exactly how to say it.

Phoebe gave him a full minute while she sprinkled a sugar substitute on her grapefruit. Then she glanced at him pointedly. "I've never known you to be so reticent about anything, Caleb. Just spit it out already so we can get on with our meal."

He met her gaze head-on. "Did you love my father?" he finally asked.

She sat back as if pushed, blinking at him for several long moments. Then, slowly, a smile spread across her face. "Is this about your father? Or about love?"

He quickly looked down at the napkin he held in his lap.

"I'll be damned. Finally."

"What?"

She waved her hand for the waiter. "I've been waiting for this talk for the past twenty years."

"What talk?"

The waiter bowed next to the table. His mother told him that they had an urgent matter to attend to and could he please arrange for the check to be billed to her room, along with a generous tip.

"But we haven't eaten," Caleb said, looking at the full table.

She ignored him as she put her own napkin on her plate and rose to her feet. "Come on. We need to find a nice, quiet spot to have this conversation...."

THE FOLLOWING MORNING at the office, Caleb was still mulling over that long-awaited conversation.

"Why did you wait so long to tell me all this?" he'd asked his mother after they'd spent several hours at his penthouse. Lionel had arranged for brunch to be served to just the two of them at a table set up in front of the floor-to-ceiling windows.

"I was waiting for you to ask, son," she'd said, warmth radiating from her blue eyes. "What I've told you today, I couldn't have shared until you were ready to hear it. And, thank God, you're finally ready...."

Caleb leaned forward and attempted to concentrate on the contract on the desk in front of him. But he'd read two words and his mind would wander again to the day before.

"I loved your father more than any other man— outside of you—in my life," she'd admitted quietly.

He'd never really asked about his father. The only conversations they'd ever had about him were always related to legitimacy issues, not matters of the heart.

"A part of me wants to say, 'Of course I loved him!' I mean, why else would I have gotten involved with a married man?" she'd asked. "I was young and naive and believed every word he said, every promise he made." Her smile had been wistful and made her look decades younger, probably much like that woman who had fallen for a married man. "And I still believe he meant both."

She'd fallen silent then, as she apparently recalled moments from that time that she would never share with anyone, not even him.

"He loved me. I know he did. But life is not always that simple. He was married and had three teenage children. When I told him I was pregnant..."

Caleb had been sitting back, coffee cup in hand, trying not to rush her.

She'd finally smiled. "When I told him I was pregnant with you, he was the happiest man in the world. He wanted both of us to take off to the west coast, leave our lives in the east behind. He would get a divorce, we would get married and we'd live happily ever after...."

She'd never told him any of this. For some reason, he'd always gotten the impression that he was the result of a one-night stand, not a full-blown love affair where promises were made, and broken.

"One week. He asked for one week to get his affairs in order. Then we would leave. We even had the tickets...."

He could have guessed the rest. One week passed and his father never made that flight, had left her sitting at the airport, alone and pregnant, with nothing but a short note saying that he was staying with his family...along with a considerable check for her to do with as she wished.

"And the checks kept coming. Every month like clockwork. Even after he passed," she'd said. "I put them all in an account for you. The account you received as a gift on the occasion of your college graduation...."

Caleb's entire reality, what he'd thought was the truth, all changed during that one conversation.

Love...

He'd had no idea that it had been connected in any way to his conception. If Theodore Winstead hadn't died would things have turned out differently? At some point, would Winstead and him have become at least friends, if not the traditional father and son?

All that was water under the bridge now.

Slowly, the contract in front of Caleb came back into focus and he looked around, having forgotten where he was. Then he reached to pick up the phone, asking Nancy to put him through to the bank where the company did all their business.

He told the account manager what he was looking for and was put on hold. Moments later, he came back on the line.

"I'm sorry, Mr. Payne, but it appears that account has been closed."

"Closed? But that's impossible."

The clicking of a keyboard and then, "No. It was closed first thing last Friday."

Bryna? Had she retrieved her funds from the escrow account after that night at her apartment?

"Could you please tell me who authorized the transaction?" he asked.

The manager shared a name with him that was not Bryna's....

"Up, up, sleepyhead...time to go to work."

Ari's voice reached Bryna in the bathroom connected to her bedroom. She tiptoed to the open doorway as he approached the bed. She hadn't made it yet, so the covers were bunched up, and apparently he thought she was still under them.

"Bryna?" he said more tentatively.

She crossed her arms over her chest.

He poked a finger at the blankets, likely expecting another groan that would send him running for the hall. Or maybe this time he was prepared for it.

"Time to get up," he said, grasping the end of the comforter in his hand.

At the same time he yanked it down, Bryna tapped him on the shoulder from behind, nearly causing him to jump out of his skin.

"Damn, Bryna! Let a guy know you're creeping up on him, will ya?"

She laughed and walked around him to make the bed. "Since you're here, make yourself useful and get the other side, will you?"

"You're dressed," he said, looking over her slacks and blouse. Not her usual work attire of skirt suit. "Good, we can ride in together."

She tugged the comforter out of his hands. "I'm not going into the office. I'm taking a sick day."

"Haven't you already taken a couple?"

She eyed him as they made quick work of the bed. "I took one. Last Friday."

"Oh. That's right. It only felt like more." They finished and he stood straight. "Would the weekend count as family sick days?"

She tossed a throw pillow at him even as she piled up the dozen or so others on top of the bed.

There. Done.

Bryna stood looking at the bed she'd spent so much of her time in over the past three days. She was glad to be out of it. While she still wasn't one hundred percent, and the ache in her chest had grown rather than diminished, at least she felt she had the energy to do something other than roll over and pull the covers above her head.

It wasn't much. But it was something.

"So," Ari said. "What do you have planned for today? Are you going to stay around the house?"

Bryna gave him a half smile. "I'm going into Seattle."

He shifted his weight from foot to foot. "To do what, exactly?"

"Wouldn't you like to know?"

"Yes, I would. Because Troy left to drive into the city, oh, about…" He glanced at his watch. "About twenty minutes ago."

Bryna grabbed the things she needed and passed Ari on her way out the door.

"Good luck," he called after her.

"Luck has nothing to do with it," she replied as she took the stairs two at a time, estimating just how fast she would have to speed in order to beat Troy to Caleb's office....

21

"YOU CAN'T LEAVE Philippidis," Palmer told Caleb as he threw the basketball at him on the private club court, hitting him hard in the chest.

Caleb dribbled the ball back and forth. The scene between him and Hasselbeck had not been a pretty one. He'd confronted him with the seizure of the account, expecting remorse. Instead, he'd received a cold smile and an explanation that he'd been directed to take it.

Directed by whom? Philippidis himself, whom Hasselbeck had admitted to reporting to since the moment Manolis had run into Bryna outside Caleb's office. He'd used information gleaned from rifling through Caleb's desk to fraudulently access the account.

The man he'd personally hired had betrayed him. Not that he was surprised. Was it so very long ago when he might have done the same thing in order to get a leg up? Hasselbeck was only looking after himself.

But he had done it at the expense of any ties with Caleb. And the first thing he had done was fire the smug bastard, since that power had yet to be taken away from him. He didn't want to see him anywhere within a mile radius of his work environment. Ever.

Now he shot the ball and missed, letting rip a string of profanities that made Palmer laugh and club members passing by stare.

"Good thing I caught you outside Hasselbeck's office or else that pent-up aggression you're showing might have ended up being directed in the wrong place," Palmer said.

Caleb guarded him, forcefully reaching around his old friend and knocking the ball from his grip.

"Whoa! Foul."

"The only rule in our games is that there are no rules." Caleb dribbled the basketball out and shot again, hitting it off the rim. "And if you think this game will stop me from confronting Philippidis, you've got another think coming."

Palmer stood still, dribbling the ball but not making any attempt at shooting. "All this over a woman?"

Anger flashed through Caleb as he stood staring at his friend. "All this over his meddling in matters that are none of his business."

"Matters concerning a woman."

"Matters concerning an independent business deal."

"With a woman. A woman with whom you were sleeping."

Caleb had never struck another person in his life and was surprised by his desire to clock Palmer.

"Whoa! Foul," his friend said for the second time, holding up his hands and backing away.

Caleb trapped the dropped ball against his side. "Tell me, Palmer. How did you happen to be at the offices to stop me from charging Philippidis, anyway?"

He hadn't considered the reason why his friend had shown up out of the blue at the time. He'd assumed he'd stopped by to invite him for a lunch b-ball session. Now he wasn't so sure.

Palmer wiped sweat from his brow with the back of his hand and then put the same hand on his hip. "I have an office there. Up the hallway from yours. Today was my first day in it." He grinned. "Looks like perfect timing."

"A little too perfect." Caleb gripped the ball in both his hands. "Since when have you had a permanent office?"

"I don't. It's not permanent," he said. "It's just until I can arrange for a place in Earnest."

Earnest. Where the Metaxases were from. Where the business deal he hoped to put together for Bryna would focus, more specifically on the Metaxas mill.

"Why Earnest?" he asked.

Palmer shrugged. "Why not Earnest?" But Caleb was having none of it. He shot the ball at him.

"Okay, okay. Earnest happens to be where I'm from." Palmer threw the ball back.

He raised a brow. "So your return has nothing to do with Philippidis."

"I didn't say that...."

Caleb rubbed his free hand over his face and then pushed his hair back. Was there nothing the Greek would stop at in order to wreak his revenge against that family?

As it was, he had dipped into his own resources to return Bryna's money to her account, his intention that she not ever know what had happened...and for him to get that same money back from Philippidis himself.

"Caleb Payne!"

His name echoed through the basketball court and commanded his complete attention. He turned to face none other than Bryna where she stood in the doorway, hands on her shapely hips.

"Your ass is mine, bud...."

BRYNA'S BLOOD PUMPED HARD through her veins, allowing her a measure of confidence that she didn't feel. At least not to the extent that she pretended.

But after having raced to Seattle at the risk of a major speeding ticket, and cutting Troy off at Caleb's offices, she was just relieved that she'd reached him before her cousin had.

The scene had been nerve-racking. Troy standing before Caleb's secretary demanding to know where he was, the possibility high that he might run into Philippidis as she had a week before. Her unsure what he wanted and unconvinced of her own ability to chase him away.

"What are you doing here?" her cousin had demanded of her.

"I could ask the same of you."

"I'm here because that son of a bitch in there did something to you that made you dive for cover in your bedroom for the past three days."

Caleb's secretary said, "Sir, I've already told you, he's not in there."

"I don't believe you."

Bryna stared at him. "What, you can't seriously think that Caleb Payne is actually afraid to see you?" she asked.

She strode toward the closed door.

"Miss Metaxas," the secretary began, getting to her feet.

But there was no need for intervention. Bryna had swung open the door, revealing an empty office.

Troy's stare could have frozen a tropical wind.

She closed the door again and went to stand in front of him. "While I'm touched by your display of…affection for me, I don't need you to fight my fights." She squared her shoulders. "I'm quite capable of fighting them myself."

"If that were true, you would never have gotten

involved with the likes of that man in the first place."

He had her there. But she wasn't going to let him know that. "What would you know about anything related to relationships, Troy? Of the man-woman variety? Last I checked, you haven't been on a date in over two years."

He cocked a brow. "I didn't realize anyone was counting."

"That's because you're incapable of seeing anything outside your hell-bent obsession with saving Earnest." She took a deep breath, knowing she was treading dangerous waters and might go under at any moment. "Did it ever occur to you that Earnest might have to take care of itself? Who died and left you savior?"

He winced at that and she immediately felt guilty. But didn't back down one iota.

"Go back home, Troy. I can handle this myself," she said more quietly. "Please."

He stared at her for a long moment and then finally his expression softened and he nodded. "You're right. I'm butting in where I don't belong."

She smiled at him.

"But if you need anything—"

"You'll be the first person I call," she'd assured him.

Who else would she turn to? The first place she'd gone when she was in desperate need of licking her wounds was the house in Earnest. The one she shared with her uncle and cousins. Home.

Thankfully, he'd left the office…and then Bryna had beseeched Caleb's secretary for his whereabouts. Surprisingly, she'd told her straight out.

And now she stood at the entrance to the private club's basketball court staring at the man in question.

How was it remotely possible that she'd forgotten how dynamic he was? The only time she'd seen him without every hair in place was in bed. But now he wore a college T-shirt and sweat pants, the soft cotton hugging his every muscle. Sweat dampened the front and the back of the shirt, and his skin color was high. His eyes glistened like black onyx, taking her in from head to foot much the same way she was him.

He looked like a dangerous predator who had just returned from a long hunt to find an unwanted animal waiting in his den. A small, defenseless animal that he could render history with one clean snap of his powerful jaws.

Why did she suddenly feel as if she'd much rather dive back under her bedcovers…?

22

THE LAST PERSON Caleb had expected to see appear in that doorway was Bryna. Yet there she stood, her glossy black hair loose around her shoulders, contrasting against her cream-colored blouse and matching slacks, the hue highlighting her naturally tanned skin.

"Speak of the she-devil," Palmer murmured.

Caleb wanted to shoot him a look of warning, but he couldn't seem to tear his gaze away from the spectacular creature striding across the court in her high heels as if she owned it. And she did. At least in that one moment. There wasn't a man alive who could be untouched by the image she cut.

A sexy female on a mission.

Then he remembered what could have made her angry enough to seek him out instead of waiting for him to return to the office or contact him via some other means: she must have discovered her money had gone missing before he'd replaced it.

She advanced on him…and kept on coming, backing him up against the wall behind the net.

"I'm sorry about the money," he said quietly, taking in her beautiful green eyes and her soft, provocative mouth, feeling an overpowering urge to kiss her.

She blinked. "What money?"

Christ, she wasn't there because of the missing resources. He grimaced. So much for keeping her from learning about the mishap.

"Are you pulling out of our professional agreement?" she asked. "For personal reasons?"

This one had a fire inside her that not even a bastard like him could extinguish. A strength that matched and might even better his.

He could barely stop himself from grinning.

"No," he said.

She propped her fists on her hips. "Then what money are you sorry about?"

"It's nothing with which to be concerned. Not anymore. Everything is as it should be."

She looked unconvinced. "Everything?"

"Mmm." God help him, if she moved any closer to him, he *was* going to kiss her.

Out of the corner of his eye he saw Palmer near them.

"You must be Miss Metaxas," his friend said, extending his hand. "I'm Palmer DeVoe."

Bryna tugged the basketball out of Caleb's hand and shoved it at him. "Nice to meet you, Palmer.

Now, if you'll excuse us, Mr. Payne and I have a few things we must discuss. Privately."

Palmer held up a hand. "Sure. Never mind me." He looked at Caleb, an amused expression on his face. "I'll just hit the showers...."

Bryna never took her gaze from Caleb.

He cleared his throat. "Would you like to go some-where...private to have this conversation?"

She squinted at him. "Why? So you can distract me with sex and then play games with me after-ward?" She shook her head. "Oh, no, buster. We're going to have this talk here and now."

One of the symptoms of love that his mother had shared with him was a painful expansion just behind the solar plexus, as if you couldn't take another breath if your life depended on it. Caleb recognized the sensation as exactly what he was feeling.

Quite simply, Bryna took his breath away.

And he'd been stupid not to admit the truth before now. Before he'd hurt her.

"I know you said you didn't love me," she began.

Her voice hitched slightly, revealing an undercur-rent of emotion she was obviously trying to keep under control.

"But I know differently."

She swallowed hard.

"I felt in my bones. Felt it in your every touch. Saw the love I was feeling reflected in your eyes. You were feeling every last emotion I was—"

"Feel," he corrected, his own throat growing unbearably tight.

Her mouth snapped shut and she searched his face. "Pardon me?"

He'd hurt this woman more than any person deserved to be hurt. All because he'd been unable to open his eyes to his own true feelings for her. He'd been a bastard for so long, he didn't know how to be anything different. A scarred child incapable of moving beyond his own imaginary constraints.

And in a strange way, it had taken hurting Bryna to finally come to terms with that. To see what love really looked like. Not just in his own heart, but in hers.

No matter what he said, what he did to her, she never blinked. She stood up against him just as she was now, determined to make him see what he'd refused to.

She was apparently waiting for him to explain himself. And he did.

"You referred to what you believed I'm feeling in the past tense. I merely corrected you."

Her eyes shone brightly as she considered his words.

Caleb couldn't help himself. He knew that she had a lot to get off her chest. But he needed to touch her.

He reached out a hand and cupped the side of her face. At her small sound of delighted surprise, emotion surged sure and strong within him. A desire he suspected would never be satisfied, no matter how many times he marked his brand on the fascinating woman before him.

"I'm sorry for what I said the other night," he whispered, wanting desperately to convince her. "I…"

She leaned her head into his palm and he suppressed a groan.

"Damn it all to hell, Bryna, I don't deserve you.…"

He watched her absently lick her bottom lip, threatening to sidetrack him.

"The truth is, I don't know much about love."

She tried to look away, but he denied her the escape.

"Even though I don't rate another chance…would you be willing to show me?"

He'd lived for so long in an emotional vacuum, consumed with his career at the expense of all else, proving himself to a father who had died long ago, he didn't know how she or anyone else was going to change that.

But it wasn't up to them to bring about a change. It was up to him. And after suffering for the better part of the past week without the touch of Bryna's skin against his, distracted to hell and back by the thought that he might never see her again, he knew he needed to make that change. Or risk becoming the type of man he despised, not respected.

To his relief and surprise, the corners of Bryna's

mouth turned up slightly into a smile and her gemlike eyes shone even more brightly. "Oh, I don't know. I think you're doing a pretty good job of it right now."

Caleb hauled her into his arms, tunneling the fingers of one hand into her hair even as he crowded her against his body with his other against her lower back. She smelled so damn good. Felt even better.

"God, I don't deserve you," he murmured, kissing her hair, then her forehead, then her nose.

She tilted her face up, her expression full of fire and need. "Don't you think I should be the one who decides that?"

Caleb's gaze moved from her eyes to her mouth and then back again. Then he finally did what he'd been hungering to since the moment he'd first spotted her standing in the doorway—he kissed her.

Any words he was unable to say he conveyed through his kiss. And he realized that it was what he'd been doing all along. While his conscious mind and lifelong hang-ups had kept him from seeing what was right in front of him, his heart and body had known all along.

A desire so strong that it blocked out everything and everyone around them took hold until a club patron cleared his throat nearby.

"Get a room," he said in disapproval.

Caleb drew his head back from Bryna, his hand pressed against her rounded bottom.

She laughed. "Where's the closest hotel…?"

Epilogue

PALMER DEVOE WAITED for Caleb outside the office building housing Philippidis's current international headquarters. The morning sunlight speared the dark rain clouds, creating a rainbow to the south. His mother might have said it was a harbinger of good things to come; of course, she'd have to be alive in order to say it. And she hadn't been around for a good long time. Too long.

That Earnest lay to the south didn't escape Palmer's attention.

Earnest…his hometown…

The place where Penelope Weaver still resided…

Caleb burst through the front doors as if they'd been blown open by a strong wind gust, his face as dark as the sky.

A scathing line of obscenities erupted from his mouth. "I could have killed the son of a bitch."

Palmer crossed his arms and considered his

longtime friend and sometime business associate from under lowered brows. "I'm guessing that went well."

Caleb paced back and forth several times, as restless as he'd ever seen him. "I never in a million years imagined I'd fall victim to a power play."

Palmer grinned, amused. "Yes, well, that's because you're usually the one making the plays."

His friend stared at him. "My point exactly."

He paced again.

Palmer weighed whether it was wise to let this play out right there or if it was better to suggest they take it to the club. He cast a long look at the building behind him and considered his own business with the man Caleb held in such low regard.

He'd never seen his friend so worked up. "You didn't do anything stupid, did you?" he asked.

Caleb stopped, aiming that glare at him.

Palmer raised his hands. "Whoa. I'm not him."

"Define *stupid*."

"Wrong choice of words. Perhaps I should have said *unprofessional*."

"Oh, what I did in there was professional, all right. I professionally told him where he could get off."

Palmer winced. Not good.

He looked back at the front doors. It probably wasn't a good idea to stick around where they could be seen in plain sight. While he sympathized with his friend's plight, he had plans of his own to implement…and that included keeping the wily Greek on his side.

"Why don't we work this out on the basketball court?" he suggested.

"I'd rather go in and clock him.…"

Palmer slapped a hand on his back and propelled him toward the street instead.

"I should have given in to the urge while I was in there."

"Probably best that you didn't. You don't want to burn any bridges."

"Burn them?" Caleb asked, a glint of humor sparking for the first time since he'd come outside. "I loaded the damn things with explosives and blew them the hell up."

Christ…

"That's right. I wouldn't work with that lowdown, scum-sucking son of a bitch again for all the money in the world. If my life depended on it. If the end of the world was nigh and he was the only one who could save me…"

Wow. Palmer put his arm loosely around Caleb's shoulders as his driver pulled up. "Don't be drastic, now."

He opened the door and Caleb climbed in the back; Palmer followed.

"I'm sure whatever happened in there isn't anything a little distance, time and clearer thinking can't fix."

Caleb squinted. "Surely you jest. Aren't you hearing a word I'm saying?"

"I'm hearing every word," he assured him. "I just don't have to like them."

Caleb paused, then asked, "You're not seriously considering continuing to work with that asshole?"

Palmer carefully weighed his words. "I'm certainly not about to dump everything I've worked so hard for over a girl."

Caleb looked ready to sock him.

He lifted his hands again. "Hey, just stating facts as I see them."

Caleb must have read something in his reaction. He drew in a deep breath and then let it out slowly, running his fingers through his hair several times before sitting back. This external manifestation of his friend's internal turmoil wasn't something he was used to seeing off the court. Caleb usually had iron-willed self-control. Most had no idea what was going on in his head.

Now you could read his every emotion like a brightly lit billboard.

"You know what?" Caleb asked. "You're right—this is about a girl."

He turned to face him; Palmer wondered if he should put up his hands to block a surprise assault.

But Caleb wasn't scowling…he was grinning.

"And it's the best damn thing I've ever done in my life."

Palmer blinked.

"Think about it," Caleb said. "When was the last time you did something that wasn't dictated by your head, but rather your heart?"

"Never," he said without hesitation.

Caleb laughed. "Me either."

This time Palmer was the one who ran his fingers through his hair, finding the unfamiliar action contagious. "You picked a helluva time to start."

"Yes, well, I think in this matter, you don't pick the time, it picks you."

He considered his friend for a long moment. "And if things don't work out?"

Caleb looked at him. "With Bryna and I?"

Palmer nodded.

He appeared to give it consideration as the car navigated the distance to the club. Finally Caleb smiled. "Then it doesn't work out."

Okay, he'd lost it.

"All I know is that I cannot not do this, Palmer. Everything in me is telling me she is the one."

Great.

A loud chuckle. "If you'd told me a week ago I'd be saying this, I'd have said you were crazy."

"Now you're the one sounding crazy."

"Maybe. But, oh, does it feel good.…"

Palmer looked out the window at Seattle, trying to get a handle on the situation. The rainbow still arced in the south. He wanted to say he had no idea how his friend felt, but the fact was, he did know…and in a few short days, he'd find out if the combination of time and distance had been enough to destroy it….

* * * * *

HARLEQUIN® *Blaze*™

COMING NEXT MONTH

Available October 26, 2010

#573 THE REAL DEAL
Lose Yourself...
Debbi Rawlins

#574 PRIVATE AFFAIRS
Private Scandals
Tori Carrington

#575 NORTHERN ENCOUNTER
Alaskan Heat
Jennifer LaBrecque

#576 TAKING CARE OF BUSINESS
Forbidden Fantasies
Kathy Lyons

#577 ONE WINTER'S NIGHT
Encounters
Lori Borrill

#578 TOUCH AND GO
Michelle Rowen

HBCNM1010

REQUEST YOUR FREE BOOKS!

2 FREE NOVELS
PLUS 2
FREE GIFTS!

HARLEQUIN®

Blaze™

Red-hot reads!

HARLEQUIN®

A Romance

FOR EVERY MOOD™

Spotlight on

Inspirational

Wholesome romances
that touch the heart and soul.

See the next page
to enjoy a sneak peek from
the Love Inspired® Suspense
inspirational series.

*See below for a sneak peek from
our inspirational line, Love Inspired® Suspense*

*Enjoy this heart-stopping excerpt from
RUNNING BLIND
by top author Shirlee McCoy,
available November 2010!*

**The mission trip to Mexico was supposed to be an
adventure. But the thrill turns sour when Jenna Dougherty
and her roommate Magdalena are kidnapped.**

"It's okay. I'm here to help." The voice was as deep as the
darkness, but Jenna Dougherty didn't believe the lie. She
could do nothing but lie still as hands slid down her arms,
felt the rope around her wrists.

"I'm going to use a knife to cut you free, Jenna. Hold
still."

The cold blade of a knife pressed close to her head before
her gag fell away.

"I—" she started, but her mouth was dry, and she could
do nothing but suck in air.

"Shhh. Whatever needs to be said can be said when
we're out of here." Nick spoke quietly, his hand gentle on
her cheek. There and gone as he sliced through the ropes on
her wrists and ankles.

He pulled her upright. "Come on. We may be on
borrowed time."

"I can't leave my friend," Jenna rasped out.

"There's no one here. Just us."

"She has to be here." Jenna took a step away.

"There's no one here. Let's go before that changes."

"It's dark. Maybe if we find a light…"

"What did you say?"

"We need to turn on the light. I can't leave until I know that—"

"What can you see, Jenna?"

"Nothing."

"No shadows? No light?"

"No."

"It's broad daylight. There's light spilling in from the window I climbed in through. You can't see it?"

She went cold at his words.

"I can't see anything."

"You've got a nasty bruise on your forehead. Maybe that has something to do with it." His fingers traced the tender flesh on her forehead.

"It doesn't matter *how* it happened. I'm blind!"

Can Nick help Jenna find her friend or will chasing this trail have Jenna running blindly again into danger?

Find out in RUNNING BLIND, available in November 2010 only from Love Inspired Suspense.

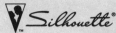